This book, the third in the original Destroyer series, is about the visit of a mythical American president to China. It first appeared in the bookstores in February 1972, the same week that Richard Nixon made his trip to China (and then spoiled it all by coming back).

That relevance was one of the charms of writing books back in the early days of *The Destroyer* series, when Pinnacle was a tiny publishing house, and deadlines were a lot more flexible. Nowadays, publishers like manuscripts in hand a year or more before a book gets published, so trying to write a novel that stays on top of the news is almost impossible.

But it wasn't just timeliness that made this book special for us. *Chinese Puzzle* was the first Destroyer in which the relationship between Remo and his teacher, Chiun, was defined, and the first book in which they actually worked together on a mission. For the first time, the legends of the House of Sinanju, the age-old house of Korean assassins, began to work their way into the stories.

Why should it take until the third book of a series to nail down such basic points as the characters, their history, and their relationships?

Well, the first Destroyer, *Created the Destroyer*, was written in 1963, but not published until 1971. In that book, Chiun was a karate instructor and nothing more. In the eight years the book was waiting for publication, karate, which had been an esoteric art in 1963, became more and more common. After publication of *Created* in 1971, we realized we needed something more, something which totally eluded us in *The Destroyer #2, Death Check*.

In *Chinese Puzzle*, we felt we had it right for the first time. This was also the book that we decided we were not going to write "splatter books," filled with bodies oozing blood, and which read like casualty reports. Instead, we decided to make humor and satire ongoing components of the series—if it lasted, which, in those days, was never certain.

Twenty-five million copies later, we're still trying to do the same thing.

—*Warren Murphy and Dick Sapir*
September 1984

The *Real* Introduction

You have just read a pack of lies, written by two idiots, and published by a third.

As usual, those two incompetent scribblers, Sapir and Murphy, have gotten everything wrong. Save one thing.

It is true that the thieving Chinese owed money to the House of Sinanju, and that I, Chiun, Master of Sinanju, collected same. Everything else is false.

I was never a karate instructor. That is like calling the sun a lightbulb. And as for these two cretins "defining" the relationship between Remo and me, they are like cockroaches who infest a house just to describe its architecture.

Even the title is wrong. *Chinese Puzzle* indeed. As all know, the true title of this book is *Chiun Collects From the Thieving Chinese*.

They call this book *Authors' Choice*. Morons' Choice would be more like it. You would all be well-advised to ignore this garbage.

With moderate tolerance for you,
I am Chiun, Master of Sinanju

AUTHORS'
CHOICE

BEST
OF

THE DESTROYER

CHINESE PUZZLE

WARREN MURPHY
RICHARD SAPIR

PINNACLE BOOKS NEW YORK

Publisher's Note

This book is the first in a series of scheduled Pinnacle reprints of the best of *The Destroyer*. While *The Destroyer* series, with more than twenty-five million copies sold, is among the bestselling action series of all time, it has grown in the last fourteen years into a cult book, read as much for its biting humor as for its action. Reviewers have called the books "flights of hilarious satire," "a mad parody on the genre," and "a brilliant commentary on our culture."

The Destroyer is all of that—and it's fun to read, too.

THE DESTROYER: CHINESE PUZZLE

Copyright © 1972 by Richard Sapir and Warren Murphy

An original Pinnacle Books edition, published for the first time anywhere.

First printing/March 1972
Twelfth printing/February 1985

ISBN: 0-523-42414-0
Can. ISBN: 0-523-43404-9

Printed in the United States of America

PINNACLE BOOKS, INC.
1430 Broadway
New York, New York 10018

For
Philip Sapir, a super-great uncle;
*Ramona, who graces worlds not good **enough for her;***
D.D., who clings to joy like a life raft.
And for Bill Ashman and Davis Jacobs
—because Remo says so.

CHAPTER ONE

He did not want coffee, tea or milk. He did not even want a pillow for his head, although the BOAC stewardess could see he was obviously dozing.

When she attempted to slip the white pillow behind his barrel neck, two younger men slapped it away and motioned her to the rear of the jet, then to the front. Any direction, so long as it was away from the man with closed eyes, and hands folded on top of a brown leather briefcase handcuffed to his right wrist.

She did not feel comfortable around this particular group of Orientals. Not with their dour faces, their cement lips obviously set in childhood never to smile.

She judged them to be Chinese. Usually Chinese were most pleasant, often charming, always intelligent. These men were stone.

She went forward to the captain's cabin, past the forward galley, where she snitched an end of a cinnamon bun and gobbled it down. She had bypassed lunch on her slimming diet and then did what she always did when she missed lunch. She ate something fattening to quell the rising hunger. Still, dieting and breaking the diet in small ways, while not really trimming pounds kept her lissome enough to hold her job.

The bun was good, somehow extra sweet. No wonder the Chinese gentleman had asked for more. Perhaps they were his favorite. Today was the first time they had served cinnamon buns. They were not even on the regular lading for the menu.

But he had liked them. She could see his eyes light when they were served. And the two men who had slapped the pillow away had been ordered to give him their buns.

She opened the front cabin door with her key and leaned into the cabin.

"Lunch, gentlemen," she said to the pilot and co-pilot.

"No," they both answered. The captain said: "We'll be over Orly soon. What kept you?"

"I don't know. It must be that time of year. Most everyone is dozing back there. I had a pickle of a bother fetching pillows. It's awfully hot here, isn't it?"

"No, it's cool," said the co-pilot. "Are you all right?"

"Yes. Yes. Just feels a bit warm. You know." She turned away, but the co-pilot did not hear her close the door. There was a good reason she did not close the door. She was suddenly sleeping, face down on the cabin floor, her skirt angling up to the pinnacle of her rump. And in those strange patterns that greet the unexpected, the co-pilot's first thought was silly. He wondered if she was exposing herself to the passengers.

He need not have worried. Of the 58 passengers, 30 had passed all cares of the world, and most of the rest were in panic.

The co-pilot heard a woman's scream. "Oh, no. Oh, no, Lord. No. No. No."

Men were yelling now also, and the co-pilot unstrapped himself and hopped over the body of the stewardess, dashing into the seat-lined body of the plane where a young woman slapped a young boy's face and kept slapping it, demanding he wake up; where a young man walked the aisle dazed; where a girl desperately pressed her ear to a middle-aged man's chest; and where two young Chinese men stood over the body of an elderly Chinese gentleman. They had drawn guns.

Where the hell were the other stews? Dammit. There was one in the back. Asleep.

He could feel the plane pitch and dive. They were going in for an emergency.

Unable to think of anything else, he yelled to the

8

passengers that they were making an emergency landing and that they should fasten their seat belts. But his voice scarcely made an impression. He dashed back to the front, pushing the dazed, wandering man down into a seat. An elderly couple nearby did not even look up. They were apparently dozing through it also.

He snatched the stewardess' microphone from its cradle hook in the small compartment near the front seat, and announced they were making an emergency landing at Orly airport and that everyone should fasten his seat belts.

"Fasten your seat belts now," he said firmly. And he saw a woman first buckle in a sleeping boy whose face she had been slapping, then resume her slapping in an effort to rouse him.

The plane moved down through the foggy night, locked in on the right path by a homing beacon that the pilot followed unerringly. Upon landing, the airplane was not allowed to taxi to the main terminal but was ordered to a hangar where ambulances and nurses and doctors were waiting. As soon as he opened the door for the platform steps, the co-pilot was pushed aside by two men in gray suits, with revolvers drawn. They went storming into the plane pushing aside two passengers. When they reached the Chinese gentleman, they returned their revolvers to their holsters, and one of them nodded to one of the young Chinese, and the two of them ran back up the aisle again, slamming into a nurse and a doctor, knocking them over, and continuing down the ground platform.

Only the people taken to the morgue or the hospital that night left the airport. It was not until midnight on the following day that the survivors were allowed to depart. They had not been allowed to see a newspaper or listen to a radio. They answered questions upon questions until all the questions and answers seemed to blend in a continuous flow of words. They talked to white men, to yellow men, to black men. And very few of the questions made sense.

Nor did the newspaper headline they were finally allowed to see:

TWENTY NINE ON FLIGHT DIE OF BOTULISM

Nowhere, noticed the copilot, did the paper mention the Chinese gentleman or his two aides, not even in the roster of passengers.

"You know, honey," he said to his wife, after reading the newspaper reports three times, "these people couldn't have died of botulism. There were no convulsions. I told you what they looked like. And besides, all our food is fresh." He said this in his small London flat.

"Well then, you should go to Scotland Yard and tell them."

"That's a good idea. Something's not on the up and up here."

Scotland Yard was very interested in his story. So were two American blokes. Everyone was so interested that they wanted to hear the story again and again. And just so the co-pilot would not forget, they gave him a room to himself that stayed locked all the time. And did not let him leave. Or call his wife.

The President of the United States sat in the large soft chair in the corner of his main office, his shoeless feet resting on a green hassock before him, his eyes riveted on predawn Washington—for him, the floodlights on the White House lawn. His pencil tapped on the sheaf of papers resting between his knees and his stomach.

His closest advisor was summing up in his professorial manner. The room smelled of the lingering cigar smoke of the CIA director who had left one hour before. The advisor spoke in the gutturals of German childhood, droning on about possibilities and probabilities of international repercussions and just why this was not as bad as it looked.

"It would not do to minimize what has happened. The

dead man was, after all, a personal emissary from the Premier. But the important thing is that the Premier's visit to this country is still on. For one thing, the emissary was not poisoned over American territory. He boarded the plane in Europe and was to transfer at Montreal, for this country. Because of this, it is apparent that the Premier does not believe that any of our people were involved. That is evident, because he has indicated a willingness to send another man to finalize the arrangements for his visit to this country."

The advisor smiled.

"Moreover, Mr. President, the Premier is sending a close friend. A colleague. A man who was with him on the long march when they were retreating from Chiang Kai Shek, and a friend who was with them in their dark days in the caves of Yenan. No, I absolutely and firmly believe, that they know we were not responsible. If they felt otherwise, they would not now send General Liu. His presence on this mission is their assertion that they believe we are of good will. So the Premier's trip will go ahead as planned."

The President sat up straight and rested his hands on his desk. It was Autumn in Washington, and the offices he entered and worked in were always toasty warm. But the desk now felt cold to the touch.

"Just how is Liu arriving?" asked the President.

"They will not let us know."

"That doesn't sound as if they are brimming over with confidence in us."

"We have not exactly been their trusted allies, Mr. President."

"But if they would let us know the route, then we could offer protection also."

"Frankly, sir, I am very happy we are unaware of General Liu's route. If we are unaware, then we are not responsible for him until he arrives in Montreal. We will hear from the Polish embassy here as to his arrival time. But he is coming. May I further stress again that they

11

informed us he would be coming, within one day of the tragedy."

"That's good. It shows they did not change policy." The table still felt cold to the touch and the President's hands felt wet. "All right. Good," he said. But there was little joy in his voice. He added, looking up: "The people who poisoned the Chinese emissary? Who could they have been? We have absolutely no clues from our intelligence. The Russians? Taiwan? Who?"

"I am surprised, Mr. President, that Intelligence did not send an entire library on who would wish the Chinese Premier not to visit the United States." He brought from his briefcase a folder the thickness of a Russian novel.

The President raised his left hand, palm forward, signalling the advisor to belay the report.

"I don't want history, Professor. I want information. Hard today information on how the Chinese security system could be breached."

"That is unavailable as yet."

"All right, dammit, then I've decided." The President rose from his chair, still clasping the sheaf of notes that had been on his lap. He put the papers down on the fine polished wood of his desk.

"On one level, we will continue with normal procedures of the intelligence and local security people. Just continue."

The advisor looked up querulously. "Yes?"

"That's it. I can't tell you anymore. I'm glad I have your services, you're doing as well as anyone could. You're doing a good job, professor. Good night."

"Mr. President, we have worked well together because you do not withhold pertinent information. At a time like this, to leave me wondering would be counterproductive."

"I agree with you 100 per cent," the President said. "However, the very nature of this area precludes my sharing it with anyone. And I'm sorry. I cannot explain further. I really cannot."

The advisor nodded.

The President watched him leave the room. The door shut with a click. Outside, the harsh floodlights would be dimmed in two hours, when replaced by the sun still steaming hot over Washington in the early fall.

He was alone, as every leader of every nation had always been when the difficult decisions had to be made. He lifted the receiver of a phone he had used only once since he had been inaugurated.

There was no need to dial although the telephone had a dial, as if it were any other telephone. He waited. He knew there would be no ringing sound on his end. There was not supposed to be. Finally he heard a sleepy voice answer.

The President said: "Hello. Sorry to wake you. I need the services of that person . . . it is a grave crisis . . . If you come down to see me then I will explain more fully . . . Yes, I must see you in person . . . and bring him, please. I want to talk to him . . . Well, then tell him to stand by for immediate service . . . All right. Fine. Yes. That would be fine for now. Yes, I understand, it's just an alert. Not a commitment. You will put him on alert. Thank you. You don't know how desperately the world needs him now."

CHAPTER TWO

His name was Remo.

He had just laced the skin-tight black cotton uniform around his legs, when the telephone rang in his room in the Hotel Nacional in San Juan, Puerto Rico.

He picked up the receiver with his left hand while finishing the cork-blackening of his face with his right. The telephone operator told him there had just been a long distance call from the Firmifex Company in Sausalito, California. The woman at Firmifex said that the shipment of durable goods would be arriving in two days.

"Yeah, okay." He hung up and said one word: "Idiots."

He turned off the lights and the room was dark. Through the open window, the sea breezes blew off the Caribbean, not cooling Puerto Rico but swirling away and redistributing some of the autumn heat. He walked out onto the open balcony with its round aluminum tube railing supported by curved metal spokes.

He was about six feet tall and the only hint of muscle was a slight thickness around the neck, wrists and ankles, but he hopped the railing to the ledge as though it were a horizontal matchstick.

He leaned into the sea slick brick wall of the Hotel Nacional, swelling its salty wetness, and feeling the cool of the ledge at his feet. The bricks were white but they appeared gray close up in the early morning darkness.

He tried to concentrate, to remember to press into the building, not away from it, but the telephone call rankled him. A 3:30 a.m. telephone call to inform him of manufacturing deliveries. What a stupid cover for an alert. They

14

might as well have advertised on prime time. They might as well have put a spotlight on him.

Remo looked down the nine stories and attempted to spot the old man. He could not. Just the darkness of the tropical shrubbery, cut by the white paths, and the rectangular splotch where the pool was, midway between hotel and beach.

"Well?" came the high-pitched Oriental voice from below.

Remo dropped from the ledge, catching it with his hands. He hung there for a moment, dangling his feet down into space. Then he began rocking his body back and forth, picking up the where of the wall, speeding his rocking, and then he opened his fingers and let go.

The swinging of his body threw him against the hotel wall, where his bare toes slid against the smooth white brick. His fingers, tensed like talons, bought a hold on the surface of the stones.

The lower half of his body rebounded out again from the wall of the hotel, and as it began to swing back in, he released his hands, and his body dropped. Again his feet braked his descent against the wall of the hotel, and again his powerful, charcoal-coated fingers pressured like talons against the wall of the Hotel Nacional.

His fingers felt the slimy Caribbean moistness on the wall. If he had tried to hang on, even momentarily, he would have plunged to his death. But he remembered the injunction: the secret is in, not down.

Remo's mind concentrated furiously on the position of his body. It must keep moving, constantly, but its force must always be inward, overcoming the downward pull of nature.

He smelled rather than felt the breezes, as he again rocked off from the wall with his legs, and dropped another five feet, before his toes and hands slowed his descent against the wall.

Fleetingly, he wondered if he really was ready. Were his hands strong enough, his timing keen enough, to over-

15

come gravity, by the disjointed rocking technique perfected in Japan by the Ninja—the warrior wizards—more than ten centuries ago?

Remo thought of the story about the man who fell from the 30th floor of a skyscraper. As he passed the 15th floor, someone inside yelled, "How are you?" "So far, so good," he answered.

So far, so good, Remo thought.

He was moving rhythmically now, an irresistible pattern of swing out, drop, swing in, and slow against the wall. Then repeat. Swing out, drop, swing in, and slow against the wall, defying gravity, defying the laws of nature, his smoothly muscled athlete's body using its strength and timing to bring its force inward against the wall, instead of down where death waited.

He was halfway down now, literally bouncing off the wall, but the downward pull was growing stronger, and as he rocked off the wall, he applied upward pressure with his leg muscles to counteract the pull.

A black speck in a black night, a professional doing professional magic, moving down the wall.

Then his feet touched the curved tiled roof of the covered walk, and he relaxed his hands, curled and rolled his body through a somersault, landing noiselessly on his bare feet on the concrete slab behind the darkened hotel. He had made it.

"Pitiful," came the voice.

The man was shaking his head, now clearly visible because of the strands of long white beard coming down from his face, the thin, almost babylike hair dotting his balding Oriental head. The whiteness of the hair was like a frame shimmering in the early morning breeze. He looked like a starvation case brought back from the grave. His name was Chiun.

"Pitiful," said the man whose head barely reached Remo's shoulder. "Pitiful."

Remo grinned. "I made it."

Chiun continued to shake his head sadly. "Yes. You

16

are magnificent. Rivalled in your skills only by the elevator which carried me down. It took you ninety seven seconds." It was an accusation, not a statement.

Chiun had not looked at his watch. He did not need to. His internal clock was unfailingly accurate, although as he approached eighty, he had once confided to Remo that he was miscalculating as much as 10 seconds a day.

"The hell with ninety seven seconds. I made it," Remo said.

Chiun threw his hands up over his head in a silent appeal to one of his innumerable gods. "The lowliest ant of the field could do it in 97 seconds. Does that make the ant dangerous? You are not Ninja. You are worthless. A piece of cheese. You and your mashed potatoes. And your roast beef and your alcohol. In ninety seven seconds, one can go up the wall."

Remo glanced up at the smooth white wall of the hotel, unbroken by ledges or handholds, a shiny slab of stone. He grinned again at Chiun. "Horsecrap."

The elderly Oriental sucked in his breath. "Get in," he hissed. "Go to the room."

Remo shrugged and turned toward the door, leading into the darkened rear section of the hotel. He held the door open, and turned to allow Chiun to pass through first. From the corner of his eye, he saw Chiun's brocaded robe vanish upward onto the top of the roof over the walkway. He was going to climb up. It was impossible. No one could climb that wall.

He hesitated momentarily, unsure if he should attempt to dissuade Chiun. No way, he realized, and walked inside rapidly and pushed the elevator button. The light showed the elevator was on the twelfth floor. Remo stabbed the round plastic button again. The light still read 12.

Remo slid into the doorway alongside the elevator, leading to the stairs. He started running, taking the stairs, three at a time, trying to gauge the time. It had been no more than 30 seconds since he had left Chiun.

He raced at full speed up the stairs, his feet noiseless on

17

the stone slabs. At a dead run, he pushed open the door leading to the ninth floor corridor. Breathing heavily, he walked to his door and stopped and listened. It was silent within. Good, Chiun was still climbing. His Oriental pride was going to get kicked.

But what if he had fallen? He was eighty years old. Suppose his twisted body lay in a heap at the base of the hotel wall?

Remo grabbed the door knob, twisted, and pushed the heavy steel door back into the room, and stepped in onto the carpet. Chiun was standing in the middle of the floor, his hazel eyes burning into Remo's dark brown eyes. "Eighty-three seconds," Chiun said. "You are even worthless for climbing stairs."

"I waited for the elevator," Remo lied, lamely.

"The truth is not in you. Even in your condition, one does not become exhausted riding the elevator."

He turned his back. There was the infernal toilet paper in his hand.

Chiun had removed a roll of toilet paper from the bathroom, and now he rolled it across the heavy rug of the hotel floor. He smoothed it down, and then reentered the bathroom. He returned with a glass of water in his hand, and began pouring it over the paper. Twice, he went into the bathroom to refill the glass, until finally the toilet paper was soaked with water.

Remo had closed the door behind him. Chiun walked over and sat on the bed. He turned to look at Remo. "Practice," he said. Almost to himself, he added: "Animals need not practice. But then they do not eat mashed potatoes. And they do not make mistakes. When man loses instinct, he must regain it by practice."

With a sigh, Remo looked across the 15-foot length of wet toilet tissue. It was an ancient Oriental training technique adapted to the 20th Century. Run along pieces of wet paper, without tearing the paper underfoot. Or, following Chiun's standards, without wrinkling it. It was the ancient art of Ninjutsu, credited to Japan but claimed by

18

Chiun for Korea. Its practitioners were called invisible men, and legend had them able to vanish in a wisp of smoke or to transform themselves into animals, or to pass through stone walls.

Remo hated the exercise, and had laughed at the legend when he first heard it. But then in a gymnasium years ago, he had fired six shots point blank at Chiun as the old man ran toward him across the floor. And all the bullets had missed.

"Practice," Chiun said.

CHAPTER THREE

No one heard the shots on Jerome Avenue in the Bronx. It was a busy time of the day and only when the black limousine with the drawn curtains spun with a crunch into one of the pillars supporting the Jerome Avenue line of the subway, did people take note that the driver appeared to be biting the steering wheel and that blood was gushing from the back of his head. The man in the front passenger's seat was resting his head on the dashboard and appeared to be vomiting blood. The curtains covering the windows of the back seat of the car were drawn and the car's engine continued to hum with the wheels locked in drive.

A gray car with four men in hats pulled up quickly behind. The men leaped from the car, guns drawn, and scrambled to the black car which churned, going nowhere, buttressed by the pillar, its nose caved in against the concrete base holding the grime-blackened steel supports of the elevated subway.

One of the four men grabbed the handle of the rear door. He tugged, then tugged again, then reached for the front door handle which also would not open. He raised his snub-nosed automatic above the handle and fired, then reached through the broken window and unlocked the rear door.

That was all Mabel Katz of 1126 Osiris Avenue, just around the corner past the delicatessen, could remember. She explained it carefully again to the attractive young man who didn't look Jewish but had a name that could be, although the FBI was not exactly the place for a young Jewish lawyer. Everyone else on the block was talking to men like these so Mrs. Katz would talk also. Although she did have to get home to make Marvin his supper. Marvin wasn't feeling well, and certainly shouldn't go without supper.

"The men in the front looked Chinese or Japanese. Maybe Viet Cong," she suggested smartly.

"Did you see any men leave the car?" asked the man.

"I heard the crash and saw some men run to the car and shoot the lock off. But there was no one inside the back."

"Did you see anyone who looked, well, suspicious?"

Mrs. Katz shook her head. What was suspicious, already, when people were shooting and cars were crashing and people were asking questions? "Will the two hurt men be all right?"

The young man shook his head. "Now did you see any Orientals around here other than the two men in the front seat?"

Mrs. Katz shook her head again.

"Do you ever see any Orientals around here?"

She shook her head again.

"What about the laundry across the street?"

"Oh, that's Mr. Pang. He's from the neighborhood."

"Well, that's Oriental."

"If you want to call him that. But I always thought Orientals meant, you know, far away and exotic."

"Did you see him near the car?"

"Mr. Pang? No. He ran out like everyone else. And that was it. Will I be on television now?"

"No."

She was not on television that night. As a matter of fact, the story was on only a few moments, and it did not mention how the neighborhood suddenly had been flooded with all sorts of investigators. It was called a tong war killing, and an announcer talked about the history of tong wars. The announcer did not even mention all the FBI men around the neighborhood or that someone in the back seat had disappeared.

Mrs. Katz was peeved when she saw the six o'clock news. But she was not quite as peeved as the man for whom she had voted. His closest advisor was also peeved:

"He was to take a motor caravan because that was the safest way to arrive here. How could he just vanish?"

Heads of departments sat almost at attention with their uniformly disastrous reports. It was a long wooden table and a long dark day. They had been there since early afternoon and although the sky could not be seen, their watches told them it was night in Washington. On the half hour, messengers brought in new reports.

The President's closest advisor pointed to a bulldog-faced man across the table. "Tell us again how it happened."

The man began the recitation, reading from notes in front of him. General Liu's car had left the caravan at approximately 11:15 a.m. and was followed by security people who frantically tried to swerve him back to the Thruway. The general's car had taken Jerome Avenue into the Bronx and another car had gotten between his car and the security auto. The security people managed to catch up to General Liu's car at 11:33 a.m., just beyond a city golf course. The car had smashed into one of the steel supports of the "el" when the security men had reached it. The general was gone. His driver and an aide were dead, shot from behind in the head. The bodies were taken to nearby Montefiore Hospital for immediate autopsy and removal of bullets, which were now being checked in ballistics.

"Enough," yelled the presidential advisor. "I am not concerned with the tedium of police details. How can we lose a person under our protection? Lose! We have lost him entirely. Didn't anyone see him? Or the people who kidnaped him? How far behind were your people?"

"About two car lengths. Another car got between them."

"Just got between them?"

"Yes."

"Does anyone know where that car went or who was in it?"

"No."

"And no one heard shots?"

"No."

"And then you found the two dead aides of General Liu and no General Liu, correct?"

"Correct."

"Gentlemen, I do not have to stress again how important this is or how deeply concerned the President is. I can only say I view this as incredible incompetence."

There was no response.

The advisor looked down the long table to a small, almost frail man, with a lemony face and large eyeglasses. He had said nothing, only taken notes.

"You," said the aide. "Do you have any suggestions?"

Heads turned toward the man. "No," he said.

"Might I be so honored as to be advised why the President asked you to this meeting?"

"No," said the man, as unruffled as if he had been asked for a match and did not have one.

The directors at the table stared at him. One squinted as if seeing a familiar face, then looked away.

The tension was broken when the door opened for the half-hourly messenger. The President's advisor stopped talking, and drummed his fingers on the stack of half-hour reports before him. Every so often a phone would light before one of the directors and he would pass on what information he had received. None had lit in front of the lemon-faced small man at the end of the table.

This time, the messenger leaned over and whispered to the aide. The aide nodded. Then the messenger went to the lemony-faced man and whispered something to him, and the man was gone.

He accompanied the messenger down a carpeted hall and was ushered into a large dark office with one lamp casting light upon a large desk. The door shut behind

23

him. He could see even through the shadows the worry on the face of the man behind the desk.

"Yes, Mr. President?" said the man.

"Well?" said the President.

"I would like to point out, sir, that I consider this whole affair rather irregular. It was an incredible breach of our operating contract for me, not only to appear at the White House but to participate in a meeting, where, I believe, for a moment I was recognized. Granted, the man who recognized me is of the utmost integrity. But that I should even be seen defeats almost every reason for our existence."

"No one knew your name besides that man?"

"That is not the point, Mr. President. If our mission becomes known, or even broadly enough suspected, then we should not have existed in the first place. Now, unless you consider what is happening important enough for us to close down our operations, I would like to leave."

"I do consider what is happening important enough for you to risk your entire operation. I would not have requested you here if I did not." His voice was tired, but not strained, a strong voice which endured and endured and endured and did not falter. "What we are dealing with today is a question of world peace. Whether or not. It's that simple."

"What I am dealing with, sir," said Dr. Harold W. Smith, "is the safety of the United States Constitution. You have the Army. You have the Navy. You have the Air Force and the Federal Bureau of Investigation and the Central Intelligence Agency and Treasury men, and grain inspectors and customs clerks and every one else. They are all within the framework of the Constitution."

"And they failed."

"What makes you think we can do any better?"

"Him," said the President. "That person."

Dr. Harold W. Smith sat silently. The President continued: "We have been in touch with the Polish Ambassador here, through whom we deal with Peking. If we do not find General Liu within one week, I am informed that as

24

much as the Premier would like to visit this country, he will not be able to. He has his nationalistic elements too. And he must deal with them. We must find General Liu."

"Then, sir, what do we need with that person you mentioned?"

"He would make the best possible bodyguard, would he not? We haven't been able to protect General Liu with quantity. Perhaps with awesome quality."

"Isn't that like putting the world's best padlock on the proverbial barn door when the horse has left?"

"Not exactly. He is going to join in the search. We are going to find General Liu."

"Sir, I have dreaded this moment. That is, when I have not longed for it."

Dr. Harold W. Smith paused to choose his words carefully, not just because he was in the presence of the President of the United States, but because a strong integrity implanted in youth insisted upon expression during manhood.

It was because of that integrity, he knew, that he had been entrusted many years before by another President. Smith then had been with the Central Intelligence Agency and had gone through three interviews with superiors in one week. All three had told him they were unaware of his potential assignment, but one, a close friend, had confided that it was a Presidential assignment. Smith immediately made a sad note of his friend's untrustworthiness. Not the written kind of note, but the constant analysis a good administrator makes. He was asked for an analysis of his three interviews on a clear and sunny morning. It was the first time he had ever spoken to a President of the United States.

"Well?" said the young man. His shock of sandy hair was combed dry. His suit was light gray and neat. He stood with a slight stoop from a recurring back injury.

"Well what, Mr. President?"

"What do you think of the people asking you questions about yourself?"

"They did their job, sir."

"But how would you evaluate them?"

"I wouldn't. Not for you, Mr. President."

"Why not?"

"Because that's not my function, sir. I'm sure you have people expert at such things."

"I am the President of the United States. Is your answer still no?"

"Yes, Mr. President."

"Thank you. Good day. By the way, you've just lost your job. What is your answer now?"

"Good day, Mr. President."

"Dr. Smith, what would you say if I told you I could have you killed?"

"I would pray for our nation."

"But you would not tell me what I asked?"

"No."

"All right. You win. Name your job."

"Forget it, Mr. President."

"You may leave," said the young, handsome man. "You have one week to reconsider."

A week later, he found himself back in the same office, refusing again to give the President the evaluation he had asked for. Finally the President spoke.

"Enough games, Dr. Smith. I have very bad news for you." His voice was no longer insinuating. It was honest, and it was frightened.

"I'm going to be killed," Smith suggested.

"Maybe you will wish you were. First, let me shake your hand and offer you my deepest respects."

Dr. Smith did not take his hand.

"No," said the President. "I guess you wouldn't. Dr. Smith, this nation will have a dictatorship within a decade. There is no question about it. Machiaelli noted that in chaos exists the seeds of dictatorship. We are entering chaos.

"Under the constitution, we cannot control organized crime. We cannot control revolutionaries. There are so

26

many things we cannot control . . . not under the constitution. Dr. Smith, I love this country and believe in it. I think we are going through trying times, but that they will pass. But I also think our government needs the help of some outside force to survive as a democracy."

The President had looked up. "You, Dr. Smith, will head that outside force. Your assignment will be to work outside the constitution to preserve the process of this government. Where there is corruption, end it. Where there is crime, stop it. Use any means you wish, short of taking human life. Help me protect our nation, Dr. Smith." The President's voice was anguished.

Smith had waited a long time before responding. Then he said: "It is dangerous, sir. Suppose I sought power to control the nation?"

"I did not exactly pick you up off the street."

"I see. I assume, sir, you have some sort of program worked out to dismantle this project if necessary?"

"Do you want to know about it?"

"If I take this assignment, no."

"I didn't think so." He passed a portfolio to Dr. Smith. "Your budgetary procedures, operating instructions, everything I could think of are in these notes. There are many details. Cover stories for you and your family. Acquisition of property. Hiring of staff. It will be difficult, Dr. Smith, since no one is aware of it but we two."

The President added: "I will tell my successor and he will tell his successor, and should you die, Dr. Smith, your organization will automatically dissolve."

"What if you should die, sir?"

"My heart is fine and I have no intention of assassination."

"What if you should be assassinated without it being your intention?"

The President smiled.

"Then it will be up to you to tell the next President."

So on a cold day, one November, Dr. Smith informed the new President of the United States of his organization.

And this time, all that President had said, was "Shoot. You mean if Ah want you to rub someone out, anyone, Ah can just say so?"

"No."

"Good. Cause for sure, Ah would have sent all you people out behind the barn to play in the daisies."

And that President had told this President, showing him the phone through which the headquarters of the secret organization, CURE, could be reached. And he had warned him that the only things a President could do was to dissolve the organization or ask for something within its mission. He could not order a mission.

And now another President was asking.

But for the light on the desk, it was dark and now the President queried, because the man before him had hesitated.

"Well?" he asked.

"I wish your people within the government could do the job."

"I wish they could too. But they have failed."

"I must seriously consider dismantling the organization," Smith said.

The President sighed. "It is very hard to be President sometimes. Please, Dr. Smith."

The President leaned into the sharp light on his desk and held his forefinger and thumb a pencil width apart. "We're this close to peace, Dr. Smith. This close."

Smith could see the tired courage in the President's face, the steel discipline pushing the man toward his goal of peace.

"I will do what you ask, Mr. President, although it will be difficult. Exposing that person as a bodyguard or even an investigator might lead to someone who knew him while he was living, recognizing his voice."

"While he was living?" the President said.

Smith ignored the unspoken question. He stood up and the President stood with him. "Good luck, Mr. Pres-

28

ident." He took the offered hand, as he had failed, and since regretted many times, to take the hand of another President years before. As he turned to walk out the door, he said: "I will assign that person."

CHAPTER FOUR

Remo was at peak. He could see the old Korean looking for the slightest wrinkle on the toilet paper and finding none, looking up in surprise. He had been training Remo for almost a solid year now since a miscalculation had kept Remo at peak for three straight months.

Remo did not wait for a compliment which would not come. In seven years of intermittent training, compliments had been rare. Remo got dressed by peeling off the ninja suit and putting on jockey shorts, white tee shirt, and covering them with slacks and a green sports shirt. He slipped into sandals, then brushed his short hair. He had gotten used to his face in the last seven years, the high cheekbones, the straighter nose, that hairline that receded just a little more. He had almost forgotten the face he used to have, back before he had been framed for a murder he did not commit and escorted to an electric chair that did not quite work, although everyone else but his new employers had thought it worked.

"Good enough," said Chiun and Remo blinked. A compliment? From Chiun? He had been acting strangely since August but a compliment for doing something right after failing so many times was incredibly strange.

"Good enough?" Remo asked.

"For a white man whose government is stupid enough to recognize China, yes."

"Please, Chiun, not that again," Remo said in exasperation. It was not that Chiun resented America recognizing Red China, he resented anyone recognizing any China. And that had caused the incidents.

Remo could not cry, but he felt moistness making demands on his eyes.

"Even for a Korean, little father?" He knew Chiun liked the title. When Remo had used it in those first days when the burns were still on his forehead and wrists and ankles where the electrodes had been placed, Chiun had rebuked him. Perhaps it had been the joking tone of voice; perhaps it was that Chiun had not believed he would live. In was back in those early days when Reno discovered the first people who also believed that, as a Newark policeman, he had not shot that pusher in an alley.

He knew he hadn't. And that was when the whole crazy life began. With the monk in to give him last rites, with a little pill on the end of his cross, asking him if he wanted to save his soul or his ass. And the pill in his mouth, and the last walk to the chair, and biting into the pill, and passing out, thinking that this was the way all condemned men were brought to the chair, by lying to them that they would be saved.

And then waking up and discovering others who knew he had been framed because they had framed him. It was really part of the price he paid for being an orphan. He had no relatives, and having none, he would be missed by no one. And it was also part of the price he paid for having been seen efficiently killing some guerillas in Vietnam.

And so he had awakened in a hospital bed with a choice. Just start some training. It was one of those beautiful little steps that could lead to anything. To a journey of a thousand miles, a lifelong love affair, a great philosophy, or a life of death. Just one step at a time.

And so CURE, the organization that did not exist, got their man who did not exist with a new face and a new mind. It was the mind, not the body, that made Remo Williams Remo Williams. Whether he was Remo Cabell or Remo Pelham or all the other Remos he had ever been. They could change neither his voice, nor his instant response to his name. But they had changed him, the

31

bastards. One step at a time. Yet he had helped. He had taken that first step, and done, albeit laughingly, the first things Chiun had taught him. Now he respected the aged Oriental as he had respected no one else he had ever known. And it saddened him to see Chiun react so un-Chiun-like to the talk of peace with China. Not that Remo cared. He had been taught not to care about those things. But it was strange that so wise a man could act so foolishly. Yet that same wise man had said once:

"One always retains the last few foolishnesses of childhood. To retain all of them is sickness. To understand them is wisdom. To abandon all of them is death. They are our first seeds of joy, and one must always have plants to water."

And in a hotel room many years from the time of that first wisdom of the little father, Remo asked:

"Even for a Korean, little father?"

He saw the old man smile. And wait. And then say, slowly: "For a Korean? I feel I must truthfully say yes."

Remo pressed on.

"Even for the village of Sinanju?"

"You have great ambitions," Chiun said.

"My heart reaches to the sky."

"For Sinanju, you are all right. Just all right."

"Is your throat all right?"

"Why?"

"I thought it hurt you to say that."

"It most certainly did."

"It is an honor, little father, to be your son."

"Another point," Chiun said. "A man who cannot apologize is no man at all. My bad temper the other night came from the relief of my fear that you would be hurt. You came down the wall perfectly. Even if it took you 97 seconds."

"You went up perfectly, little father. And even more quickly."

"Any schmuck can do a perfect up, my son." Chiun had been picking up those Jewish words again. He learned

32

them from the elderly Jewish ladies he liked to converse with, discussing their common interest: their betrayal by their children and the personal misery ensuing therefrom.

Mrs. Solomon was Chiun's latest. They met every day for breakfast in the restaurant that faced the sea. She would repeat how her son had sent her to San Juan for a vacation and did not phone, even though she had waited by the phone the entire first month.

Chiun would confide that his most loved son of 50 years ago was doing an unspeakable thing. And Mrs. Solomon would put a hand to her face in shared shock. She had done it for the last week and half. And Chiun had yet to tell her the unspeakable thing.

It was fortunate, Remo had thought, that no one laughed at the pair. Because there would surely be a laughter with an extra thoracic cavity.

It had almost come to that the day the young Puerto Rican busboy had sassed Mrs. Solomon for saying the bagels were not fresh. The busboy was the amateur middleweight champion of the island and was just holding the job at the Nacional until he turned professional.

One day he decided he did not want to be a professional. It was approximately the time he saw the wall coming at him, and the unfinished bagel going seaward.

Mrs. Solomon had personally registered a complaint about the young ruffian attacking a fine, warm, sweet, old man. Chiun had stood there in innocence as the ambulance attendants carried the unconscious busboy out of the dining area and into the ambulance.

How had the young man attacked the elderly gentleman? asked the Puerto Rican police.

"By leaning, I think," Mrs. Solomon said. That was definitely what she thought. After all, Mr. Parks certainly would not have reached across the table and thrown the person into a wall. Why, he was old enough to be her ... well, uncle.

"I mean, there was this snort from that young man and the next thing I saw, well, I guess, he was like kissing the

33

wall and falling back down. It was very strange. Will he be all right?"

"He'll recover," a policeman said.

"That's nice," said Mrs. Solomon. "It will certainly make my friend feel better."

Her friend had bowed in his Oriental way. And Mrs. Solomon thought that was just adorable for a man carrying the burden of a son who had done an unspeakable thing. Remo had been forced to give Chiun another lecture. They had become more frequent since the President had announced plans to visit Red China.

They had sat on the beach as the Caribbean sky became red, then gray, then black, and when he felt they were alone, Remo had scooped a handful of sand and let it sift through his fingers, and said: "Little father, there is no man I respect like you."

Chiun sat quietly in his white robes, as though breathing his salt content for the day. He said nothing.

"There are times that pain me, little father," Remo said. "You do not know who we work for. I do. And knowing that, I know how important it is that we do not attract attention to ourselves. I do not know when this retraining will end and we will be separated. But when you are with me. . . . Well, we were very lucky that the busboy thinks he slipped on something. We were lucky in San Francisco also last month. But as you yourself have told me, just as luck is given, it is taken away. Luck is the least sure of all events."

The waves made steady slapping sounds and the air began to cool. Softly, Chiun said something that sounded like "kvinch."

"What?" said Remo.

"Kvetcher," said Chiun.

"I do not know Korean," said Remo.

"It is not Korean, but is apt anyway. Mrs. Solomon uses the word. It is a noun."

"I assume you want me to ask you what it means."

"It is of no matter. One is what one is."

34

"All right, Chiun. What is a kvetcher?"

"I do not know if it translates that well in English."

"Since when are you a rabbinical student?"

"This is Yiddish, not Hebrew."

"I'm not auditioning you for Fiddler on the Roof."

"A kvetcher is one who complains and complains and worries and complains over the slightest little nothing."

"That busboy will not walk without crutches for months."

"That busboy will no longer be abusive. I have given him an invaluable lesson."

"That he should never be off balance when you're in one of your moods?"

"That he should treat the elderly with respect. If more youngsters respected the elderly, the world would be a far more tranquil place. That has always been the trouble with civilization. Lack of respect for age."

"You're telling me that I should not talk to you like this?"

"You hear what you will hear and I say what I will say. That is what I am telling you."

"I may have to terminate this training because of what happened," Remo said.

"You will do what you will do and I will do what I will do."

"Will you not do what you have done?"

"I will take into account your nervousness over a nothing."

"Were those football players a nothing?"

"If one wants to worry, he will find no shortage of subjects."

Remo threw up his hands. Invincible ignorance was invincible ignorance.

Later, the phone rang. Probably the signal to abort. Of 10 alerts a year, if Remo went into action once, it was a lot.

"Yes," said Remo.

"Nine o'clock tonight in the casino. Your mother will

be there," said the voice. And then the receiver clicked down.

"What the hell?" Remo said questioningly.

"Did you say something?"

"I said a bunch of idiots are acting pretty peculiar."

"The American way," said Chiun happily.

Remo did not answer.

CHAPTER FIVE

The casino was like a large living room with anxious muffled sounds and subdued lighting. Remo arrived at 9 p.m. He had checked his watch 45 minutes earlier and was checking to see how close he could come to approximating minutes. Forty-five minutes was perfect because it came to exactly three short times, the units of time upon which Remo had built his judgment.

He looked at the second hand of his watch when he entered the casino. He was 15 seconds off. Which was good. Not up to Chiun, but still good.

Remo wore a dark double-breasted suit with a light blue shirt and dark blue tie. His shirt cuffs were double buttoned. He never wore cufflinks since extraneous metal hanging from his wrist by threads could never be controlled.

"Where are the smallest bets allowed?" Remo asked a tuxedoed Puerto Rican whose aplomb showed he worked there.

"Roulette," said the man, pointing to two tables along a wall, surrounded by a gaggle of people identical to the other gaggles of people surrounding other tables. Remo moved easily through the crowd, spotting a pickpocket at work, and casually grading his technique. His moves were too jerky; he was barely adequate.

His ears picked up an argument over the size of bets and he was fairly certain by its nature that Dr. Smith was in it.

"Minimum bet is one dollar sir," repeated the croupier.

"Now I purchased these 25 cent chips and you sold

them to me, thus making a mutual contract. Your sale of a 25 cent chip commits you to allowing 25 cent bets."

"At times we do. But now we do not, sir. The minimum bet is one dollar."

"Outrageous. Let me speak to the manager."

There was a small whispered conference of the two casino men at the table.

Finally, one said, "If you wish, sir, you may cash in your chips now. Or, if you still insist, you may bet 25 cent chips."

"All right," said the bitter faced man. "Go ahead."

"Are you going to make your wager now?"

"No," said the man, "I want to see first how the table is running."

"Yes sir," said the croupier, called all bets and spun the wheel.

"Good evening, sir," said Remo, leaning over Dr. Smith and brushing his jacket ever so gently. "Losing?"

"No, I'm seventy five cents ahead. Wouldn't you know that as soon as someone starts to score on them, they try to change the rules?"

"How long have you been here?"

"An hour."

"Oh." Remo pretended to take from his pocket the wad of bills he had just extracted from Dr. Smith's pocket. He glanced through it. There was more than two thousand dollars. Remo bought mounds and mounds of $25 chips. Two thousand dollars worth. He blanketed the table with them.

"What are you doing?" demanded Dr. Smith.

"Betting," Remo said.

The ball bounced and spun and clinked to a hard stop. The croupiers almost instantly began collecting chips and paying off bets. Remo almost broke even.

And again he spread out his money in bets. He did this five more times as he saw the controlled anger well in Dr. Smith. Since Remo was obviously a lunatic, the croupiers did not enforce the house limit of $25 a number on him. So on the sixth roll, Remo had $100 on number 23 when it came out, and he collected $3,500 on the bet.

He cashed in his chips and left with Dr. Smith behind him. They entered the hotel's night club where the noise would be loud and where, if they sat up front and faced the noise, they could talk without being overhead. Talking into noise provided an excellent sound seal.

When they were seated, to all eyes apparently watching the bouncing breasts bathed in neon and incredible metallic costumes, Dr. Smith said:

"You gave that man a $100 tip. A one hundred dollar tip. Whose money did you think you were betting?"

"Oh," Remo said, "I damn near forgot." He took the roll of bills from his pocket, and counted off $2,000. "It was your money," he said. "Here."

Smith patted his pocket, felt it empty, and took the money without further comment. He changed the subject.

"You're probably wondering why I am meeting you directly, without setting breaks in the chain."

Remo had been wondering just that. His original go was to be an advertisement in the morning paper, whereupon he would catch a flight to Kennedy Airport—the first after 6 o'clock in the morning. He would then go to the men's room nearest the Pan Am counter, wait till it was empty and then say something to himself about flowers and sunshine.

A wallet would be handed out from one of the toilet stalls. He would check the wallet to make sure the seal on it was still intact. If it wasn't, he would kill the man in the stall. But if the seal was not broken, he would exchange his current wallet, and leave without ever letting the man see his face. Then he would open the new wallet and not only get his new identity, but also the meeting place with Smith.

This was the first time Smith had ever contacted him directly.

"Yes, I was wondering."

"Well, we don't have time to discuss it. You will meet a

Chinese woman at Dorval Airport in Montreal. Your cover will be that you are her bodyguard, assigned by the United States Secret Service. You will stay with her as she looks for a General Liu. You will help her find him, if you can. There are only six days left to do it. When General Liu is found, you will stay with him and protect his life also, until both of them return safely to China."

"And?"

"And what?"

"What is my assignment?"

"That is your assignment."

"But I'm not trained as a bodyguard. That's not my function."

"I know."

"But you were the one who stressed that I should only fulfill my function. If I wanted to do something else for the government, you suggested that I volunteer to help collect garbage. That's what you said."

"I know."

"Doctor Smith, this whole thing is stupid. Incompetent."

"In a way, yes."

"In what way, no?"

"In the small distance we are from having the beginning of peace. A lasting peace for mankind."

"That's no reason to switch my function."

"That's not your decision."

"It's one goddam beaut of a way to get me killed."

Smith ignored him. "And one more thing."

"What else?"

The trumpet blare ceased as a new act with soft music floated onto the stage in another aspect of undress. The two men at the table stared forward, silent, until the blaring resumed.

"You will take Chiun with you. That is why I am meeting you here. He is to function as your interpreter, since he speaks both the Cantonese and Mandarin dialects."

40

"Sorry, Dr. Smith, that busts it. No way. I can't take Chiun. Not on anything to do with the Chinese. He hates the Chinese almost as much as he hates the Japanese."

"He's still a professional. He's been a professional since childhood."

"He's also been a Korean from the village of Sinanju since childhood. I've never seen him hate before, not until this business of the Chinese Premier coming to the U.S. But I'm seeing it now, and I know he also taught me that competence decreases with anger." In Remo's vocabulary, incompetence was the vilest word. When your life depends on the correct move, the greatest sin is "incompetence."

"Look," Smith said, "Asians are always fighting among themselves."

"As opposed to who?"

"All right. But his family has taken Chinese contracts for ages."

"And he hates them."

"And he would still take their money."

"You're going to get me killed. You haven't succeeded yet. But you'll make it."

"Are you taking the assignment?"

Remo was silent for a moment as more young, well-formed breasts set over well-formed butts, topped by well formed faces paraded out in some symmetrical dance step to the brassy blaring of the trumpets.

"Well?" said Smith.

They had taken the human body, the beautiful human body, and packaged it in tinsel and lights and noise and made the parading of it obscene. They had aimed at the exact bottom of human taste, and were right on target. Was this garbage what he was supposed to give his life for?

Or maybe it was freedom of speech? Was he supposed to stand up and salute for that? He didn't particularly want to listen to most of the things said anyway. Jerry Rubin, Abbie Hoffman, the Rev. McIntyre?

What was so valuable about freedom of speech? It just

was not worth his life to let them mouth off. And the constitution? That was just a bunch of rigamarole that he had never quite trusted.

He was—and this was Remo's secret—willing to live for CURE but not to die for it. Dying was stupid. That's why they gave people uniforms to do it in and played music. You never had to march people into a bedroom or to a fine dinner.

That was why the Irish had such great fighting songs and great singers. Like, what was his name, the singer with the too loud amplifiers in that club on third Avenue. Brian Anthony. He could make you want to march with his songs. Which is why, as any intelligence man knew, the IRA couldn't compare to the Mau Mau or any other terrorist group, let alone the Viet Cong. The Irish saw the nobility in dying. So they died.

Brian Anthony and his big happy voice and here Remo was listening to this blare when his heart could be soaring with the boys in green. That was what dying was good for. Singing about, and nothing else.

"Well?" said Smith again.

"Chiun's out," said Remo.

"But you need an interpreter."

"Get another."

"He's already been cleared. The Chinese intelligence people have his description and yours as Secret Service men."

"Great. You really take precautions, don't you?"

"Well? Will you take this assignment?"

"Aren't you going to tell me that I can refuse and no one will think any the worse of me?"

"Don't be absurd."

Remo saw a couple from Seneca Falls, New York that he had seen before with their children. This was their night of sin, their two weeks of living placed gem-like in the 11½ month setting of their lives. Or was it really the other way around, the two weeks only reinforcing their real enjoyment? What difference did it make? They could have children, they could have a home, and for Remo Williams there would never be children or a home, because too much time and money and risk had gone into producing him. And then he realized that this was the first time Smith had ever asked—asked instead of ordered—him to take an assignment. And for Smith to do that, the assignment meant something, perhaps to those people from Seneca Falls. Perhaps to their children yet to be born.

"Okay," said Remo.

"Good," said Dr. Smith. "You don't know how close this nation is to peace."

Remo smiled. It was a sad smile, a smile of oh-world-you-put-me-in-the-electric-chair.

"Did I say something funny?"

"Yes. World peace."

"You think world peace is funny?"

"I think world peace is impossible. I think you're funny. I think I'm funny. Come now. I'll take you to your flight."

"Why?" asked Smith.

"So you get back alive. You've just been set up for a kill, sweetheart."

CHAPTER SIX

"How do you know I've been set up?" Smith asked as their taxi sped down the multi-laned highway to San Juan Airport.

"How're the kids?"

"The kids? What do . . . ? Oh."

Remo could see the driver's neck tense. He kept whistling the same dull tune he had begun as soon as they had left the Nacional. He undoubtedly thought the whistling would show he was relaxed and carefree and not at all part of the set-up Remo had seen form, first in the casino, and then in the nightclub. They had all telegraphed, just as the driver was telegraphing now. With them, it had been never letting their eyes settle on Remo or Smith, while continuing to move as though Remo and Smith were at one of the loci of an ellipse. It was a feel Chiun had taught Remo's senses. Remo practiced in department stores by picking up objects and holding them, until he sensed that feel from a manager or a sales clerk. The difficult part wasn't really sensing when you were the object of scrutiny. It was knowing when you were not.

The driver whistled away in his classic telegraph. The same tune with the same pitch over and over. He had dislocated his thoughts from the sound; it was the only way he could reproduce the same sound over and over. His neck was red with dark potholes like tiny moon craters, filled with perspiration and grime. His hair was heavily greased and combed back in rigid black sticks that looked like the framework of a germ nursery.

The new aluminum highway lights cut through the humidity like underwater flashlights. It was the Caribbean and it was a wonder that the poured concrete foundations of the large American hotels did not go moldy along with the will of the people.

"We'll wait," Dr. Smith said.

"No, that's all right," Remo said. "The car's safe."

"But I thought. . . ." said Smith, glancing at the driver.

"He's all right," Remo said. "He's a dead man."

"I still feel uncomfortable. What if you should miss? Well, all right. We are compromised now. The fact that I am followed shows we are known. I'm not sure how much these people know, but I do not believe it is everything. If you understand."

The driver's head had begun to twitch, but he said nothing, intimating that he was not listening to the conversation behind him. His hand reached slowly toward the microphone of the two-way radio Remo had spotted on entering the taxi. He had been sure it was off.

Remo leaned forward over the seat. "Please don't do that," he said sweetly, "or I'll have to tear your arm out of its socket."

"Wha?" said the cab driver. "You crazy or something. I gotta phone in to the dispatcher."

"Just make the turnoff to the side road without telling anyone. Your friends will follow you."

"Hey, listen, Mister. I don't want trouble. But if you want it, you can have it."

His black eyes darted to the mirror, then back to the road. Remo smiled into the mirror and saw the man ease his right hand away from the radio to his belt. A weapon.

It was the new sort of taxi now being introduced into New York City with a bullet proof glass slide that the driver can move into place by pressing a button near his door. The doors locked from the front, and only a little microphone and a money slot connected the driver and his passengers.

Remo saw the driver's knee move and touch the hidden switch. The bullet proof shield slid quickly up into place. The locks clicked on the rear doors.

The bullet proof window had one flaw. It ran inside a metal track.

"I can't hear you too well," Remo said, and with his fingers peeled off the aluminum track from the body of the cab. The window dropped and Remo carefully set it at Smith's feet.

Remo leaned forward again. "Look, fella," he asked, "can you drive with just your left hand?"

"Yeah," said the driver. "See?" And with his right hand, he brandished a snub-nosed .38 caliber pistol.

Smith appeared mildly interested.

"That's nice," said Remo, as he grasped the driver's shoulder in his right hand, insinuating his thumb into the mass of bunched muscle and nerve. The driver lost control of his arm, then his hand, then his fingers, and they opened, dropping the gun quietly onto the rubber-matted floor.

"That's right," Remo said, as if talking to a baby. "Now just turn off where you're supposed to turn off so the cars behind can ambush us."

"Uhh," the driver moaned.

"Listen," Remo said. "If they get us, you live. A deal?"

"Uhh," responded the driver through clenched teeth.

"Yes, I thought you'd feel that way." He squeezed the driver's shoulder again, evoking a shriek of pain. Smith looked upset; he did not like these activities except on written reports. "This is the deal," Remo told the driver. "You stop where your friends want you to stop. And if we die you live. Okay?"

He lightened the pressure on the shoulder and the driver said "Right. You got a deal, gringo."

"Are you sure that's wise?" Smith asked.

"Why kill someone you don't have to?"

"But he's the enemy. Perhaps we should just dispose of him, grab the car and run?"

"You want me to get out now and let you handle it?"

"No," said Dr. Smith.

"Then if you would, sir, shut up."

46

Just before a green sign directing them to the airport, the driver turned right onto what appeared to be a long black unlit road, penetrating a misty green swamp. He drove for a mile, then turned off onto a dirt road underneath hanging trees. It was a dark green misty night.

He stopped the engine. "This is where you die, gringo."

"It's where one of us dies, companero," Remo said. Remo liked him, but not so much that he didn't knock him out by releasing his shoulder, leaning forward, and driving a hard index finger into his solar plexis. Okay, Remo thought. Good for at least two minutes.

Two sedans began to pull up behind them, parking ten feet behind the cab, side by side.

Remo could see their onrushing headlights in the mirror and then they stopped. He pressed Smith's head down roughly. "Stay on the floor," he growled. "Don't try to help."

He slid out of the right hand door. Four men poured out of each car, one group approaching the back of the cab from the left, the other from the right. Remo stood behind the cab, between the lines of the eight men, his hands resting behind him on the cab's trunk.

"You're all under arrest," he said. The eight stopped.

"What's the charge?" one of them answered, in precise English. In the light of the headlamps, Remo could see he was a tall heavy man with a bony face, wearing a snap brim hat. His answer marked him as the group's leader. That was what Remo wanted to know. He had use for him.

The man repeated, "What's the charge?"

"Reckless dying," Remo said. He leaned his weight back onto his hands, then with a push of his arms and a leap his lower body flashed through the air. The polished tip of his right shoe crashed into the Adam's apple of the first man on his right. His feet hit the ground, his hands still on the trunk of the cab, and without stopping, he spun about on the trunk of the car and repeated the action, flashing out with his left foot at the man closest to him on the left. This shoe too was christened in the Adam's apple. The action had occurred so quickly that both men fell simultaneously, their throats crushed, death on its way.

Remo moved off the trunk of the cab in between the three-man rows, and the six men charged. One fired a shot, but Remo made it miss, and it landed in the stomach of a man charging from the other side. He teetered, then fell heavily.

The remaining men moved together in a kaleidoscope of arms and legs and bodies, flailing, reaching out for Remo. They dropped their weapons in the close quarters, hoping to use their hands. But their hands captured only air, and Remo moved through them, in the classic patterns 1500 years old, as if travelling through a different dimension of space and time. Their hands closed on air. Their lunges enveloped each other. None touched Remo and he spun through them, performing the ancient secrets of aiki, the escape art, but aiki made deadly through performance by a killing machine.

He fractured a skull here, perforated a kidney there, with an elbow crazed a temple into shattered jaggers of bone.

Six were down and done. Two were left, including the leader. Remo moved directly now and faster because if they regained their composure, they would know he was a clear target for their bullets. Pulling his blows, he knocked out the two remaining men with hiraken blows to the side of the head.

He propped the two living men against the back of the cab and called "Doctor Smith."

Smith's head appeared in the rear glass of the cab, then he climbed out through the door Remo had left open.

"Look around," Remo said. "Recognize anyone?"

Smith looked at the two men that Remo had propped up against the trunk of the cab. He shook his head. Then he walked around, through the glare of the two cars' headlights, turning over men's bodies with a toe, bending closer sometimes to see a face. He walked back to Remo.

"I never saw any of them," he said.

Remo reached up and touched his thumbs to the temples of the two men, and gave a rotating squeeze. Both groaned their way into consciousness.

He allowed the leader to be aware of the man on his left. Then Remo leaped into the air, and came down full force with a steely elbow on the top of the man's skull. Just as quickly, Remo brought out gray bloodish matter in his hand.

"You want to go like this?"

"No," said the leader.

"Okay. Who sent you?"

"I don't know. It was just a contract from the states."

"Good night," said Remo and sent the man on his eternal way by driving a knee into the man's right kidney.

He and Smith walked to the front of the cab. The driver moaned.

"Can we let him live?" Smith asked.

"Only if we hire him."

"I can't do that," said Smith.

"Then I've got to kill him."

"I knew these things had to be done, but. . . ."

"You wipe me out, sweetheart. What do you think those numbers I phone in mean?"

"I know. But they were numbers."

"They were never numbers."

"All right. Do what you must do. World peace."

"It's always so easy to say," said Remo. He looked into the driver's black eyes. "I'm sorry, companero."

The man's addled mind began to sort the fact of the gringo still alive, and he said: "You deserve to live, gringo. You deserve."

"Good night, companero," Remo said softly.

"Good night, gringo. Perhaps another time over a drink."

"To another time, my friend." And Remo saluted the driver with death.

"Are you sure he's dead?" Smith asked.

"Up yours," Remo said, and pushed the driver's body out of the car and got behind the wheel. "Get in," he said roughly.

"You don't have to be rude."

Remo started the car and backed over a few bodies in steering around the two parked cars, back onto the black road. He picked up speed and turned onto the road to the airport. He did not drive as other men did, either too quickly or puttering slowly along. He maintained a computer-even pace on springs he did not trust and with an engine in whose power he had little faith.

The car smelled of death. Not decayed death but a smell Remo had learned to recognize. Human fear. He did not know if it had come from the driver, or if it came now from Smith who sat quietly in the rear seat.

When he pulled up to the airport, Smith said, "It's a business that makes you sick sometimes."

"They would have done the same to us. What makes you sick is that we live on others' deaths. I'll see you again, or I won't," Remo said.

"Good luck," said Smith. "I think we're starting without the element of surprise."

"Whatever would make you believe that?" Remo asked, and laughed out loud as Smith took his luggage and departed.

Then Remo drove back to the Nacional.

He would still have to face Chiun. And it might have been easier for him to die on the side road.

But again, as the little father had told him: "It is always easier to die. Living takes courage."

Did Remo have the courage to tell Chiun that he would be instrumental in bringing about peace with China?

CHAPTER SEVEN

She was a very little girl in a very big gray coat from which her delicate hands poked out, lost in the immensity of the cuffs. The two hands clutched a little red book.

She wore big rimmed round eyeglasses that reinforced her oval eggshell face and made it appear even more frail and more loveable. Her black hair was neatly combed back and parted in the center.

She appeared no older than 13 and was definitely airsick and probably frightened. She sat in the front of the BOAC jet, not moving, determinedly looking forward.

Remo and Chiun had arrived at Dorval Airport in Montreal less than a half hour earlier. Chiun had gone onto the jet first, hiding behind a business suit and a gold badge of identification. As soon as they had brushed past the stewardess, Chiun pointed to the sick little girl and said:

"That's her. That's the beast. You can smell them."

He went to the girl and said something in what Remo assumed was Chinese. The girl nodded and answered. Then Chiun said something that was obviously a curse, and showed his identification to the girl.

"She wishes to see yours also, this little harlot of the pig sty. Perhaps to steal it. All her people are thieves, you know."

Remo showed his identification and smiled. She looked at the picture on his ID, and then at Remo.

"One can never be too careful," she said, in excellent English. "Would you please show me to the room for women? I am rather ill. But I shall overcome it. Just as I overcome the rudeness and reactionary vilification of your running dog."

"Dung of dung," answered Chuin. His hazel eyes blazed hate.

The girl managed to lift herself up and Remo helped her down the gangway steps as she struggled under the coat. Chiun followed uncomfortably. He wore black American shoes and his beard had been shaved close. He had shocked Remo back at the Nacional in San Juan when Remo had first posed the question. But Remo should have known that by now he should not be shocked by Chiun.

"I can read English also," said the girl. "To destroy imperialism, one must know its language."

"Good thinking," Remo said.

"You may be an iron tiger in the short run, but you are a paper tiger in the long run. The people are the iron tiger in the long run."

"Can't argue with that," Remo said. "That's the ladies room," he said, pointing to a sign she had missed on her march from the gangway.

"Thank you," she said and handed him the little red book. "Treasure this with your life."

"Sure thing," Remo said, taking the plastic bound book. Then she spun as if on parade and, still entrapped in the large gray coat, marched into the ladies room. Remo could have sworn he saw her take toilet paper from her pocket before she entered.

"You are already reading the propaganda of that little wanton seducer," said Chiun, looking triumphantly and at the same time disdainfully at the book.

"She's just a kid, Chiun."

"Tiger cubs can kill. Children are the most vicious."

Remo shrugged. He was still grateful that Chiun had come. And still surprised. After all, there was the San Francisco incident.

They had been bringing Remo's mind and body along slowly after an overpeak that almost became a burnout, when the President announced the impending visit by China's Premier.

52

Chiun was already disturbed because the Wonderful World of Disney had been preempted for the President. Remo was working on his deep breathing, looking out at the Golden Gate Bridge, trying to see himself running across its suspension bands and breathing accordingly.

Chiun had worked Remo back into shape very well and very quickly, which was not surprising since he had devoted his life to that sort of thing, starting his own training at 18 months. When he had begun training Remo, he had informed him that he was 26 years too late to do anything serious but he would do the best he could.

Mentally, Remo was going down the far side of the Golden Gate bridge, when he heard a shriek.

He quickly floated into the living room. Chiun was making hostile, oriental sounds at the television set from which the President spoke in his usual dull and precise manner, always appearing more sincere when he abstained from trying to show warmth or joy.

"Thank you and good night," said the President, but Chiun would not let the image escape, and he fractured the picture tube with a kick of his foot, the main tube imploding on itself before showering the room with splinters.

"What did you do that for?"

"You fool," said Chiun, his wispy beard quivering. "You pale faced fool. You imbecile. And your president. White is the color of sickness and you are sick. Sick. All of you."

"What happened?"

"Stupid happened. Stupid happened. You are stupid."

"What did I do?"

"You did not have to do anything. You are white. That is deed enough."

And Chiun returned to the console to smash the wood top of the set with his left hand, and with his right hand caved in the right side, leaving the left corner of the cabinet rising like a steeple. For that, he smashed his elbow down, shattering it into splinters.

He stood in front of the split wiring and wood and shards of glass and triumphantly spit down upon it.

"China's Premier is visiting your country," he said, and spit again.

"Chiun. Where is your sense of balance?"

"Where is your country's sense of honor?"

"You mean you're for Chiang Kai Shek?"

Chiun spit again at the remains of the television set. "Chiang and Mao are two brothers. They are Chinese. You cannot trust the Chinese. No man should trust Chinese who wishes to keep pants and shirt. The fool."

"You have something against the Chinese?"

Calmly Chiun opened his hand and looked at his fingers. "My, you are perceptive tonight. My training has done well by you. You perceive even the faintest vibration. You soar to ultimate understanding."

"Okay, Chiun. Okay. Okay."

But it was not okay.

The next night, while passing the third Chinese restaurant, Chiun spat for the third time.

"Chiun, will you cut that out?" Remo whispered, and for a reply, drew a deft elbow in the solar plexus that might have sent an ordinary man to a hospital. Remo let out a grunt. His pain seemed to make Chiun feel better because Chiun began humming as he shuffled along, waiting for the next Chinese restaurant to spit at.

Then it happened.

They were big, perhaps the biggest bulk of men Remo had ever seen up close. Their shoulders were at the tip of his head, and they stretched broad and wide, their bodies came down straight and sturdy like three large cigarette machines. Their shopping bag size heads were connected to their shoulders by what medically would be called necks, but more accurately were only swollen growths of muscle tissue.

They wore blue blazers with Los Angeles Bisons patches on them. There was one crew cut, a greasy longish job, and an Afro. They must have weighed nearly a half ton.

The stood there in front of the glass window of the furniture store singing in harmony. Training camp had obviously ended and they were out for a night on the town. When in good and joyous faith, made more joyous by booze, they accosted a wizened old Oriental, none of them had intended at the time to end his professional football career.

"Hail, brother of the third world," sang out the giant with the Afro.

Chiun stopped, his delicate hands resting, clasped before him. He looked at the black man and said nothing.

"I hail the President's decision to welcome your premier, a great leader of the third world. The Chinaman and the black man are brothers."

Thus ended the wonderful career of defensive tackle Bad Boulder Jones. The newspapers the next day said that in all probability he would be able to walk again within a year. His two companions were suspended for a game and fined $500 each. They both insisted to the police and to the press that a little old Chinaman had picked up Bad Boulder and thrown him at them.

Coach Harrahan, according to the press, said that he was not really a strict coach, but this sort of heavy drinking was ruinous to a team. "It has already permanently injured one of the great defensive tackles in football history. It is a tragedy, compounded by an obvious lie."

While the coach was sorting his problems, Remo was sorting his own. He was getting Chiun the hell out of San Francisco and on to San Juan, where one night he was forced to ask a favor he thought Chiun would never grant.

Chiun was resting in his suite where he was listed as Mr. Parks and Remo as his manservant. Smith had just gotten off to a safe return to headquarters. The only way to ask it was to ask it.

Remo asked it.

Chiun. We must guard the life of a Chinese person, and attempt to save the life of another."

Chiun nodded.

"You will do it?"

"Yes, of course. Why not?"

"Well, I know how you feel about Chinese, that's all."

"Feel? What is there to feel for vermin? If our lords who pay our sustenance wish us to watch and protect cockroaches, then we do just that."

Chiun smiled. "Just one thing," he said.

"What is that?" Remo asked.

"If we are supposed to get any money from the Chinese, get the money first. Before you do anything. Just the other day, they hired some people from my village and had them do most dangerous tasks. They not only did not pay them, they attempted to dispose of them."

"I didn't know the Chinese Communists hired the people of your village."

"Not the Communists. The emperor Chu Ti."

"Chu Ti? The one who built the forbidden city?"

"The same."

"What do you mean, the other day? That was 500 years ago."

"A day in the memory of a Korean. Just be sure we get paid first."

"We will." Remo was again surprised when Chiun willingly agreed to trim his beard for the assignment.

"When you deal with vermin, it makes no difference how you look," Chiun had said.

And now they waited outside the ladies' room at Dorval Airport. The late September rain played on the windows and had cut chillingly through their light summer suits. They would have to purchase fall clothes as soon as possible.

"She is probably robbing the washroom of soap and towels and toilet tissue," said Chiun, smiling.

"She's been in there ten minutes. Maybe I'd better check," Remo said.

So taking out his Special Services badge which came with the identities Remo and Chiun had been given by Smith, Remo stormed into the ladies' room, announcing "Health inspector, ladies. Be just a minute." And since the tone was correct and officially distant, no one had protested but left quickly.

All but her. She was piling up paper towelling and stuffing it in her great coat.

"What are you doing?" Remo asked.

"There may be no towels or paper in your country. There is plenty here. Plenty. Paper in every stall."

"There's paper all over the United States in every stall."

"In every stall?"

"Well, except when someone forgets to fill them up."

"Aha. Then we take a little. I brought some with me from Peking."

"Toilet paper?"

"Preparedness for a task is the doing of the task. He who does not prepare a task by looking at it from many sides is destined to stumble on one side. Be prepared."

"You a girl scout?"

"No. The thoughts of Mao. Where is the book?" She looked at him anxiously.

"It's outside with my partner."

"Have you read it yet?"

"I've only had it ten minutes."

"Ten minutes can be two most valuable thoughts of Chairman Mao. It could liberate you from your imperialistic, exploitative ways. And also your running dog."

Remo grabbed the young girl firmly but gently by both shoulders.

"Look, kid," he said. "I don't care what names you use for me. If it gives you kicks, all right. But watch what you call Chiun. 'Running dog' and 'imperialist lackey' are not fitting words for a man three or four times your age."

"If the old is reactionary and decadent, it must be

buried, along with all the other anachronisms afflicting mankind today."

"He's a friend of mine," Remo said. "I don't want him hurt."

"Your only friends are the party and your worker solidarity."

The young girl said that, waiting for approval. She did not expect two sharp stinging pains under her armpits. Remo kept his thumbs working, rotating, pressing the flesh up into the joint. Her delicate almond eyes went almost round with pain. Her mouth opened to scream and Remo switched one hand to her mouth.

"Listen kid and listen close. I do not want you insulting that man outside. He deserves your respect. If you are unable to give that, at least you may avoid disrespect. I would suggest that he knows more about the world than you and if you would just shut up for a moment, you might learn something from him.

"But whether you do or not is no concern of mine. What concerns me is your lack of manners, and if you mouth off just one more time, kid, I'm going to grind your shoulders into mush."

Remo pressed his right thumb in even deeper and felt her body tighten even more. Her face contorted with pain.

"Now we have had our little dialogue," Remo said, "and we have formed our revolutionary consensus. Correct?"

He released the hand from her mouth. She nodded and gasped.

"Correct," she said. "I will show the old man respect. I will take one step backwards, so that I may take two steps forward at a later date. I am allowed to speak the truth to you, however? Without fear of aggression?"

"Sure, kid."

"You are a shithead, Remo whatever-your-name-is."

She had begun to rebutton her great coat, using maximum energy on each large button. She had obviously

58

remembered his name from the identity cards Remo and Chiun had flashed.

"Not an imperialistic, oppressive, reactionary, fascistic shithead?"

"A shithead is a shithead."

"All right, Miss Liu."

"My name is Mrs. Liu."

"You're married to the general's son?"

"I am married to General Liu and I am looking for my husband."

Remo remembered the small picture from briefing. General Liu's face was hard and weatherbeaten, with strong lines cut in the bitterness of many long marches. He was 62 years old.

"But you're a kid."

"I am not a kid, damn you. I am 22 and I have the revolutionary consciousness of someone three times my age."

"You have the body of a kid."

"That's all you decadent westerners would think about."

"General Liu didn't marry you for your revolutionary consciousness."

"Yes, he did, as a matter of fact. But you wouldn't understand that." She buttoned the top button with defiance.

"Okay, let's go. Look, I can't call you Mrs. Liu for obvious reasons. You can't travel under that name either. It's already been proved we've got a system like a sieve. What do I call you?"

"Lotus Blossom, shithead," she said with ringing sarcasm.

"Okay, don't be funny," said Remo, holding open the door of the ladies' room and receiving stunned stares from passersby.

"Mei Soong," she said.

Chiung was waiting with his hands behind his back. He was smiling sweetly.

59

"The book," said Mei Soong.

"You treasure the book?"

"It is my most valued possession."

Chiun's smile reached for the outer limits of joy and he brought his hands before him, containing paper shreds and red plastic shreds, the remnants of the book.

"Lies. They are lies," he said. "Chinese lies."

Mei Soong was stunned.

"My book," she said softly. "The thoughts of Chairman Mao."

"Why did you do that, Chiun? I mean, really Chiun. That's really rotten. I mean there was no reason to do that to this little girl's book."

"Ha, ha, ha," said Chiun, gleefully and threw the pieces into the air, raining the thoughts of Mao in very small pieces over the entrance to the ladies' room of Dorval Airport.

Mei Soong's soft lips began to crinkle and her eyes moistened.

And Chiun laughed the louder.

"Look, Mei Soong, I'll get you another little red book. We have loads of them in our country."

"That one was given me by my husband at our wedding."

"Well, we'll find him and we'll get you another one. Okay? We'll get you a dozen. In English, Russian, French and Chinese."

"There are none in Russian."

"Well, whatever. Okay?"

Her eyes narrowed. She stared at the laughing Chiun and said something softly in Chinese. Chiun laughed even more. Then he said something in return in the same language. And Mei Soong smiled triumphantly and answered. Each response, back and forth, became louder and louder until Chiun and Mrs. Liu sounded like a tong war in a tin kettle.

They raved on that way at each other, the elderly man the young woman, as they departed the gates of Dorval

Airport with ticket clerks, passengers, baggage men, everyone turning to stare at the two shriekers. Remo desperately wished he could just run away, and trailed behind pretending he did not know the two.

Above was a balcony packed three deep with people staring down at the trio. It was as if they had box seats to a performance.

And Remo, in despair, yelled up at them:

"We'll go to any lengths for secrecy."

CHAPTER EIGHT

Dr. Harold W. Smith read the reports that came in hourly. If he had gone home to sleep, they would be stacked a foot high in the small safe that was built into the left side of his desk. If he stayed in his office at the Folcroft Sanitarium overlooking Long Island Sound from the Westchester shore, they would be brought into his office and quietly placed in front of him by an assistant.

That assistant believed he worked on a scientific program so hush-hush that it did not have a name. Smith's personal secretary was under the impression she worked for the Federal Bureau of Investigation on a special undercover team.

Of the 343 employees at Folcroft Sanitarium, the majority believed they worked for a sanitarium, although there were very few patients. A large portion of the employes were certain they knew. Because of computer banks underground, they were certain they worked for an international scientific-marketing firm.

One employee, an ambitious young genius, had attempted to crack the computer's program for his own personal use. He reasoned that if he could gain access to the secrets of the giant computer bank, then he could use his information to make a fortune in the market, or in international currency. After all, why such secrecy unless the secrets were worth fortunes?

Being a bright fellow, he realized the secrets must be worth fortunes because, on just a rough estimate, it cost Folcroft $250,000 a week to operate.

So in little steps he began to make contact with other facets of the computer operations, in addition to the section in which he quite legitimately worked.

And within a year he began to see a picture emerging—of hundreds of employees gathering information, of profiles of criminal networks, espionage, business swindles, subversion, corruption. A computer portrait of illegal America.

It definitely was not marketing, although his small computer function had led him to believe that since it dealt with the New York Stock Exchange.

It puzzled him. It puzzled him all the way to his new assignment in Utah. Then one night, it struck him exactly what Folcroft was about. It struck him approximately 24 hours before he met a man in Salt Lake City. A man whose name was Remo.

For a day, he was the third employee of CURE who knew for whom he worked and why. And then he was intertwined with the shock absorbers at the bottom of an elevator shaft, and only two employees, Dr. Smith and a man named Remo, knew for whom they worked and why. Which was the way it was supposed to be.

Now the hourly reports were showing that perhaps the danger of exposure was imminent again, something that Smith had dreaded since the early formation of CURE years before.

He had dozed at his desk the night before, and awoke with the first salmon shimmers in the cold gray dawn, crowning the darkness of Long Island Sound. His one-way window to the sound collected early morning dew around the edges although he had been assured that the thermal windows would not do such a thing.

His assistant had just quietly deposited another report in front of him when Smith opened his eyes.

"Bring me my electric razor and my toothbrush, please," he said.

"Certainly," said the assistant. "That special clearing section is working very smoothly, sir. I must say this is the first information clearing center to work so smoothly while not knowing what it was doing."

"The razor, please," Smith said. He turned the bundles

of reports in front of him over, and began to look through them chronologically. The reports were apparently unrelated documents, which was as it should be. Only one person should be able to put the pieces together.

A salesman for a car company in Puerto Rico reported on the love life of the owner of a cab company. An accountant, believing he was being bribed by the Internal Revenue Service, made note of a sudden large deposit of money by the owner of the cab company.

A doorman, where a young woman kept her pet poodle, told a newspaper reporter who had paid for the poodle.

A flight from Albania to Leipzig, then Paris. Large amounts of money coming out of Eastern Europe in small bills. An according upgrading of CIA activities, in case the money was payment for increased espionage.

But the money came in through Puerto Rico. And the taxicab company. And Smith remembered the bodies strewn out behind the cab on the lonely side road near the airport.

And then disturbing reports.

The Chinese girl arriving at Dorval Airport. Met by an elderly Korean and a bodyguard. The bodyguard, six feet tall, brown eyes, well-tanned complexion, medium build.

And there it was. The photograph. Of Remo Williams walking behind Chiun and the girl.

And if he could be photographed by the Pelnor Investigative Service which believed it serviced an industrial account in Rye, New York, who else could make solid contact with the trio and the only other employee of CURE who knew for whom he worked?

That photograph alone was like sighting a gun, not only at Remo Williams' head but at CURE itself.

To be known. To be exposed. The armor of secrecy peeled off. And the fact that the United States government itself could not function within its own laws, laid bare.

If the Pelnor Investigative Service could so easily spot the trio, who else?

There it was, the two Orientals obviously yelling at each other, and the man who had been publicly executed years before. A neat picture obviously shot with a not-very-long telephoto lens.

The face of Remo Williams had been changed by plastic surgery, the cheekbones, nose and hairline altered. But to see their ultimate weapon, The Destroyer, in a common photograph made by simple private detectives made Smith's already queasy stomach turn sour in anticipation of coming doom.

CURE would be disbanded before being exposed. Only the two men would know, as they had known before, and they would not know for long. Smith had prepared the destruct mechanism the day he returned from his meeting with the President.

He had his pill. He would phone his wife and tell her he was off on business. In a month, a man from the C.I.A. would tell Mrs. Smith her husband had been lost on an assignment in Europe. She would believe it because she still believed that he worked for the C.I.A.

Smith dropped the photograph into the shredder basket behind him. The basket whirred and Remo Williams' picture disappeared.

He spun his chair around and peered out at the sound and the lapping waves breaking over the rocks in small rhythmic currents, dictated by moon and wind and tide.

The water was there before CURE. It would be there after CURE. It had been there when Athens was a democracy, when Rome was a republic, and when China stood at the center of world civilization, known for its justice and wisdom and serenity.

They had fallen and the water continued. And when CURE was gone, there would still be the water.

Smith would do several small things when he put CURE into destruct. He would make the phone call to payroll which would reassign approximately half the people back to the agencies they thought they worked for anyway, turn Folcroft back into a real sanitarium, and dismiss with recommendations the remainder.

When this large scale dismissal was processed through the computer, it would set off in one day a raging fire within the computer complex destroying the tapes and the equipment.

Smith would not witness the fire. He would have, 24 hours earlier, left a memo ordering shipment of a box in the basement to the Maher Funeral Home in Parsippany, New Jersey. He would not see the memo executed either.

He would have gone downstairs, to the corner of the paint room, where the box stood in the corner, slightly taller and wider than the average man. He would remove the light aluminum lid, lie down in the tight white foam rubber, approximately hollowed for his figure, and pull the lid back down over himself. From the inside, he would snap shut four locks that fastened the lid and made it airtight.

He would need no air. Because when the last lock was closed, he would swallow the pill and go to sleep forever along with the organization he had helped design to save a nation incapable of saving itself.

What of Remo Williams? He would die soon after if the plan worked. And it was the only plan that could work. For when Smith had put the destruct plan on "prepare", Remo's executioner was already at Remo's side. He had been assigned to accompany him.

Smith would receive the daily phone contact from Remo through a Detroit dial-a-prayer, and would tell Remo to send Chiun back to Folcroft immediately.

And when Remo told this to Chiun, Chiun would fulfill his contract of death, as Koreans had been fulfilling contracts for centuries.

And Remo and Smith would carry with them to their graves the awesome secret of CURE. And when the only other person who even knew of its existence called from the White House, he would get that busy signal on the special line signifying that CURE was no more.

66

Chiun, who never knew for whom he worked except that it was the government, would probably return to Korea to live his few remaining years in peace.

The waves beat steadily on the shore.

The world was close to peace. What a fantastic dream. How many years of peace had the world known? Was there ever a time when man was not killing man, or when war upon relentless war was not being waged to adjust this border or to right that wrong, or even in its ultimate silliness, to protect a nation's honor?

The President had a dream. And Smith and Remo might have to die for it. So be it. It was worth dying for.

It would be nice to be able to tell Remo why he was going to die but Smith could not dare reveal how Remo would die. If one had an advantage against this most perfect killing machine, one kept it. To use when needed.

And then the special line from Remo rang.

Smith picked up the receiver. He suddenly felt a deep and disturbing affection for this wisecracking killer, the sort of attachment one makes in a foxhole one has shared with someone for . . . what was it now, eight years?

"Seven-four-four," said Smith.

"You're some piece of work," came Remo's voice. "You really gave me the business. You know the two of them are fighting?"

"I know."

"It's incredibly stupid to keep Chiun on this thing. He's popped his cork."

"You need someone who can translate."

"She speaks English."

"And what does she speak to a Chinese who might try to contact her?" Smith said.

"Okay. I'll try to live through it. We'll be leaving Boston later today."

"We're checking out that Puerto Rican group. We still don't know who sent them."

"Okay. We're going to start looking around."

"Be careful. That cab company has delivered a very fat

little bundle of cash to the mainland. I think it's for you, $70,000."

"Is that all I'm worth? Even with the deflated dollar?"

"If that doesn't work, you'll probably be worth $100,-000 soon."

"Hell, I'm worth that to a medicine show. Or a sports contract. How would that be if everything comes apart? A 35-year old cornerback who retires at sixty? Chiun could play tackle. I bet he could. That would blow their minds. An eighty-year-old, ninety-pound tackle."

"Stop the foolishness."

"That's what I like about you, sweetheart. You're all joy."

"Goodbye," said Smith.

"Chiun. The ninety-pound Alex Karras."

Smith hung up and returned to the reports. They were all bad and getting worse. Perhaps his own fear of dying was now clouding his judgment. Perhaps CURE already had passed the point of compromise. Maybe he should have ordered Chiun back to Folcroft then and there.

From the safe on the left side of his desk, he withdrew a small air-sealed plastic bag. It held one pill. He put it in his vest and went back to the reports. Remo would contact again tomorrow.

The new reports were coming in again, this time with his razor. Remo's call line had been tapped and traced to Rye, New York. That information came from an assistant traffic manager of a telephone company in Boston.

Smith flicked the intercom to see if his secretary was in yet.

"Yes, Dr. Smith," came the voice over the intercom.

"Oh. Good morning. Please send a memo to the shipping department. We're almost certainly going to send an aluminum box of laboratory equipment to Parsippany, New Jersey, tomorrow. I'd like it routed through Pittsburgh and then flown in."

CHAPTER NINE

Ricardo deEstrana y Montaldo y Ruiz Guerner had told his visitor that $70,000 was not enough.

"Impossible," he said, strolling to his patio, his velvet slippered feet moving silently over the fieldstone. He walked to its edge and rested his breakfast champagne on the stone ledge separating him from his acres of rolling gardens that became forest, and beyond that, the Hudson River about to be enveloped in the glorious bright colors of fall.

"Just impossible," he said again, and breathed deeply the grape-scented breeze coming from his arbors nestling in the New York hills, good wine country because the vines must fight for survival among the rocks. How like life, that its quality was a reflection of its struggle. How true of his vineyards, which he personally supervised.

He was well into middle age, yet exercise and the good life left him remarkably trim and his continental manners and immaculate dress provided his bed with constant companionship. When he wanted. Which was always before and after, but never during the harvest.

Now, this grubby little woman with a purse full of money, obviously some sort of Communist affiliate, and more than likely just a messenger, wanted him to risk his life for $70,000.

"Impossible," he said for the third time and lifted the glass from the hard rock edge of his patio. He held it to the sun as a thank you and the tinted bubbling liquid glistened, as if honored to be chosen for an offering to the sun.

Ricardo deEstrana y Montaldo y Ruiz Guerner did not

face his guest, to whom he did not offer champagne just as he had not offered her a seat. He had met her in his den, heard her proposition, and declined it. Yet she did not leave.

Now he heard her heavy shoes follow him, clomping out onto his patio.

"But $70,000 is more than twice what you get ordinarily."

"Madame," he said, his voice cold with contempt. "Seventy thousands dollars is twice what I received in 1948. I have not been working since then."

"But this is an important assignment."

"For you perhaps. Not for me."

"Why won't you take it?"

"That is simply none of your concern, Madame."

"Have you lost your revolutionary fervor?"

"I have never had a revolutionary fervor."

"You must take this assignment."

He felt her breath behind him, the intense heat of a nervous sweaty woman. You could feel her presence in the pores of your skin. That was the curse of sensitivity, the sensitivity that made Ricardo deEstrana y Montaldo y Ruiz Guerner percisely Ricardo deEstrana y Montaldo y Ruiz Guerner. Once, at $35,000 a mission.

He sipped his champagne, allowing his mouth to surrender to its vibrancy. A good champagne, not a great one. And unfortunately, not even an interesting champagne although champagnes were notoriously uninteresting anyway. Dull. Like the woman.

"The masses have bled for the success which is imminent. The victory of the proletariat over the oppressive, racist capitalist system. Now join us in victory or die in defeat."

"Oh, piffle. How old are you, Madame?"

"You mock my revolutionary ardor?"

"I am shocked at a grownup's addiction to it. Communism is for people who never grow up. I take Disneyland more seriously."

70

"I cannot believe that you would say such a thing, you who have fought the fascist beast."

He turned to examine the woman more closely. Her face was lined with years of rage, her hair cast scraggly in many directions beneath a plain black hat that could use a cleaning. Her eyes seemed tired and old. It was a face that had lived through a lifetime of arguments about the absurdities of dialectical materialism and class consciousness, far from where human beings lived their lives. She was about his age, he believed, yet appeared old and worn as though beyond the reach of even a spark of life.

"Madame, I fought the fascist beast, and so, am qualified to speak on it. It is identical to the communist beast. A beast is a beast. And my revolutionary fervor died when I saw what was supposed to replace the oppression of fascism. It was the oppression of such dullards as yourself. To me, Stalin, Hitler and Mao Tse Tung are identical."

"You have changed, Ricardo."

"I should hope so, Madame. People do grow up, unless stunted by some mass movement or other group sickness. I take it you knew me before?"

"You do not remember me?" Her voice, for the first time, wore some warmth.

"No, I do not."

"You do not remember the seige at Alcazar?"

"I remember that."

"You do not remember the battle at Teruel?"

"I remember that."

"And you do not remember me?"

"I do not."

"Maria Deloubier?"

The champagne glass shattered on the fieldstone terrace. Guerner's face paled.

"Maria," he gasped. "You?"

"Yes."

"Gentle, sweet Maria. No."

He looked at the haggard, cold face with the old eyes

71

and he still could not see Maria, the young woman who believed and loved, who had reached out each morning for the sunshine as she reached out for a new world.

"Yes," said the old woman.

"Impossible," he said. "Time does not ravage like that, without leaving a trace."

"When you give your life to something, your life goes with it."

"No. Only if you give your life to something without life." Ricardo deEstrana y Montaldo y Ruiz Guerner gently placed his left hand on the woman's shoulder. He could feel the coarseness of the material, over the hardness of the bone.

"Come," he said. "We will eat. And we will talk."

"Will you do this thing for us, Ricardo? It is so important."

"We will talk, Maria. We have much to talk about."

Reluctantly, the woman agreed, and during the morning repast of fruit and wine and cheese, she answered questions about where she went after this cell collapsed, or that revolution succeeded, or this agitation failed or that one succeeded.

And Guerner discovered where Maria had fled, leaving only this passionless woman before him. Maria was the classic revolutionary, so involved with masses and power structures and political awareness that she forgot human beings. People became objects. Positive responses meant Communists, negative responses meant not Communist.

So it was easy for her to lump Nazis together with monarchists, democrats, republicans, capitalists. To her they were all alike. They were "them." He also found that she had never remained in a country where her revolutionary efforts were successful. Those who dream most of the promised land are the ones most afraid to cross its borders.

Maria had softened as she shared the wine. "And what of you, Ricardito?"

"I have my vines, my estate, my land."

72

"No man owns land."

"I own this land as much as any man owns anything. I have changed this land and these changes are mine. Its beauty is nature. Which I might add does very well without the help of a revolutionary committee."

"You no longer use your skill?"

"I use it in different ways. Now I create."

"When you left us, you worked for others also, no?"

"Sometimes."

"Against the revolution?"

"Of course."

"How could you?"

"Maria, I fought for the loyalists for the same reason many fought for the fascists. It was the only war around at the time."

"But you believed. I know you believed."

"I believed, my dear, because I was young. And then I grew up."

"I hope then that I never grow up."

"You have grown old without growing up."

"That is unkind. But I would expect that of someone who could pour a life into a hillside instead of giving it to mankind."

Guerner threw back his leonine head and laughed.

"Really. That is just too much. You ask me to kill a man for $70,000 and you call it serving mankind."

"It is. It is. They are a counter-revolutionary force that we have been unable to overcome."

"Does it not strike you as odd that they sent you to me with the money?"

"You once had a reputation."

"But why now?"

The woman cupped her harsh reddish hands around the goblet as she had done when she was young and soft and beautiful, when the wine was not that good.

"All right, Ricardito. We will follow your thinking because you are the only one capable of thinking. And everyone else, especially a committee, cannot match your wisdom."

"Your organization has many people who effectively eliminate others. True?"

"True."

"Then why after more than 20 years must they choose a mercenary? Do they think I would not speak if captured? Absurd. Or do they plan to kill me afterwards? Why bother? They could get someone else, for much less than $70,000. Someone more politically reliable and less likely to need extermination. True?"

"True," said Maria, drinking more of the wine and feeling its warmth.

"They obviously chose me because they know they might not succeed with their own people. And how would they know this? Because they have tried before and failed. True?"

"True."

"How many times have they tried?"

"Once."

"And what happened?"

"We lost eight men."

"They seem to have forgotten my specialty in the assassination of one man. At the most, two."

"They are not forgetful."

"Why then do they expect me to attack a company?"

"They do not. It is a man. His name, as best as we can learn, is Remo."

"He killed eight men?"

"Yes."

"With what weapon? He must be very fast and select his range of fire brilliantly. And of course, he is accurate."

"He used his hands as near as we can tell."

Guerner put down his goblet. "His hands?"

"Yes."

He began to chuckle. "Maria, my dear. I would have done it for $35,000. He is perfect for my weapon. And easy."

74

Ricardo deEstrana y Montaldo y Ruiz Guerner threw back his head again and laughed. "With his hands," he said. "A toast to a man who is fool enough to use his hands." They toasted again but the woman took merely a formal sip.

"One more thing, Ricardo."

"Yes?"

"I must accompany you."

"Impossible."

"They wish to make sure that everything is done neatly. There is a Chinese girl who is not to be killed. Just the man and possibly his elderly companion."

She withdrew a picture from the purse she had kept on her arm all the while, even while eating.

"These are the men to die. The Caucasian definitely. And this girl is to live."

Guerner took the photograph between two fingers. It was obviously shot from above, with a telephoto lens. Because of the absence of depth of field and the obvious fluorescent lighting which would allow an f.4 opening, Guerner estimated the lens to be .200 millimeter.

The Oriental man was elderly, his wraithlike arms waving above him in gesture to the young girl. Behind him came the younger Occidental with the look of frustration. His eyes were deepset, his cheekbones slightly high, his lips thin and his nose strong but not large. Average build.

"The Oriental is not Korean?"

"No. She is Chinese."

"I mean the man."

"Let me see," said Maria, taking back the picture.

"I don't know," she said.

"No doubt they all look alike to you, my revolutionary friend."

"Why does it matter?"

"It would matter if he were a certain type of Korean. But that is doubtful. Keep the picture. I have it in my mind."

He whistled gently that afternoon as he removed a long

tubular black leather case from the locked safe behind his family's coat of arms.

With a chamois cloth, he polished up the rich blackness of the leather, then folded the cloth and put in on the oak desk by the window. He placed the leather case beside the cloth. The afternoon sun made white flashes on the leather. Guerner placed a hand on either side of the case, and with a snap, it opened, revealing a Monte Carlo stock made of highly glossed walnut, and a black metal rifle barrel two feet long.

They rested on purple velvet, like machined jewels for the elegance of death.

"Hello, darling," whispered Guerner. "We work again. Do you wish to? Have you rested too long?"

He stroked the barrel with the tips of his right fingers.

"You are magnificent," he said. "You have never been readier."

"You still talk to your weapon?" Maria was laughing.

"Of course. Do you think a weapon is purely mechanical? Yes, you would. You think people are mechanical. But it is not. They are not."

"I only asked. It seemed . . . somehow . . . strange."

"It is stranger, my dear, that I have never missed. Never. Is that not strange?"

"It is training and skill."

Blood rushed to Guerner's aristocratic face, filling the cheeks like a child's coloring book.

"No," he said angrily. "It is feeling. One must feel his weapon and his bullet and his target. He must feel it is correct to shoot. And then the path of the bullet is correct. Those who miss do not feel their shots, do not carefully insert them into their target. I do not miss, because I feel my shots into my victim. Nothing else is important. The wind, the light, the distance. All are meaningless. You would more easily miss picking your cigarette up from the ashtray than I would miss my target."

Guerner then began his ritual, leaving the weapon unassembled in the case. He sat at the desk and rang for his butler by pulling a cloth cord that hung from the high beamed ceiling.

He hummed softly as he waited, not looking at Maria. She could never understand. She could not feel. And not feeling, she could not learn how to live.

The door opened and the butler entered.

"Thank you, Oswald. Please bring me my supplies." Only seconds later, the butler reentered bearing another black leather case, similar to a doctor's bag.

As he carefully emptied the bag onto the desk, Guerner spoke. "Those who buy ammunition and expect uniformity are incredibly foolish. They buy approximation and therefore attain approximation. The expert must know each bullet."

He picked up a dullish gray slug from the desk and rubbed it between his fingers, feeling his finger oil coat the projectile. He stared at the bullet, absorbing its feel and its shape and weight and temperature. He placed it before him at the right of the desk. He picked up dozens of slugs, one at a time, putting most of them back into the black leather bag, and finally choosing four more which he placed with the first.

From a small wooden box on the desk, he selected a cartridge casing, held it momentarily, then replaced it. He took another, held it, rolled it between his fingers, and smiled.

"Yes," he murmured, and placed it with the slugs. He continued until he had five. "Perfect," he said. "Created to be joined together. Like man and woman. Like life and death."

With a small silver spoon, he began to ladle a white powder carefully into each cartridge. It swished in silently, a few grains at a time, giving each shell its explosive charge. When he had finished, he delicately placed a slug into the open end of each shell, and then placed them one at a time into a chrome plated device, which sealed them with a faint click.

"Now the cartridge, the bullet, the powder are one. Along with the maker. We will soon be ready."

Lifting the rifle barrel carefully from the case, he held it silently before him, peered through it, then put it down. He lifted out the stock, hefting it, holding it in firing position at his shoulder. With a soft murmur of approval, he placed the barrel on top of the stock and with a specially-tooled wrench began joining the two.

He stood up, extending his weapon from him in one hand. "We are done," he said, and inserted a bullet into the chamber, and pushed forward the bolt with a click.

"Only five bullets? Will that be enough for this job?"

"There are only two targets. Two bullets are enough for this job. The other three are for practice. My weapon and I have been inactive for so long. Get the binoculars. Behind you. On the shelf."

Guerner moved to the window, looking out over his valley, rolling lawns in front, the last blooming garden off to his right. The autumn sun was dying red over the Hudson beyond, bathing the valley in blood.

Maria picked up the 7x35 Zeiss Ikon binoculars from the shelf and noticed there was dust on the lenses. Strange. He worshipped that rifle as if a woman, and let a fine pair of binoculars gather dust. Well, he had once been very good.

She walked to the open window by him and felt the late afternoon chill. A bird sang harshly off in the distance. She wiped the binocular lenses clean on her sleeve and did not notice that this drew a glance of contempt from Guerner.

He looked forward out the window. "Two hundred yards from here," he said, pointing, "there is a small furry animal. I cannot see it too clearly."

She raised the binoculars to her eyes. "Where?"

"About ten yards to the left of the corner of the stone wall."

She focused on the wall and was surprised that through the lenses, the wall appeared better lit than to her naked eyes. She remembered this was characteristic of good binoculars.

"I can't see it," she said.

"It's moving. Now it's still."

Maria scanned the wall, and there perched on its hind legs, its forelegs tucked in front as though begging, was a chipmunk. She could barely make it out.

"I know what you're doing," she said, still looking. "You know little animals are always on that wall and when you shoot it will hide and you will say you shot it."

Maria felt the crack of the rifle at her left ear, just before she saw the chipmunk spin over as though slapped in the head with a paddle, a ball of orange fur bouncing backwards, rolling out of sight behind the wall, then rolling into sight again, the legs just as they had been, but without a head. The legs quivered. The white patch on the stomach still pulsated.

"That bird," said Guerner quietly and Maria again heard the painful crack of the rifle, and suddenly in a flock of dark birds far in the distance, perhaps 300 yards, one dropped. And she did not lift her binoculars because she knew its head was gone too.

"Another chipmunk," Guerner said, and the rifle cracked, and Maria saw nothing, partly because she had stopped looking.

"It is only possible if the target is alive," Guerner said. "That is the secret. One must sense the life of the target. One must feel it move into the orbit of your life. And then, there can be no miss."

He clutched his rifle to his chest, as though thanking the instrument.

"When do we perform against this fool this Remo who uses only his hands?" he asked.

"Tomorrow morning," Maria said.

"Good. My weapon can hardly wait." He squeezed it tenderly in his two large hands. "The target, the living target, gives itself to you. We want the living target to do

79

it with. The secret is that you do it with the victim." His voice was smooth and deep and vibrant. As it had been 30 years before, Maria remembered, when they had made love.

CHAPTER TEN

Seventy thousand dollars. How did they arrive at that price? Remo hung up the phone in the booth and walked out to Adams Street.

The sun made Boston alive, a very dead city from the time the first settler designed the dirty, gloomy metropolis, to this September noon when the air was warm with just a hint of growing coolness.

He had done his morning exercises behind the wheel of the rented automobile, driving all night from Montreal to the din of Chiun and the young Mrs. Liu. At one point, while he was reinforcing his breathing, Mrs. Liu surrendered to angry tears. Chiun leaned forward and whispered in Remo's ear: "They don't like that. Heh, heh."

"Chiun, will you cut that out now?" Remo said.

Chiun laughed and repeated the phrase in Chinese that had caused the anger.

"My government has sent me here to officially identify my husband," Mei Soong said in English. "They did not send me here to suffer abuse from this reactionary, meddlesome old man."

"I show you how old I am in bed, little girl. Heh, heh."

"You are gross, even for a Korean. Do you still remember your last erection?"

Chiun emitted a warlike shriek and then poured forth verbal Oriental abuse.

Remo pulled to the side of the road. "All right, Chiun. Up front with me."

Stilled instantly, Chiun moved into the front seat and adjusted himself angrily. "You are a white man," he said. "Like moldy dead grain. White."

81

"I thought you were mad at her, not me," Remo said, pulling back to the Thruway where cars were zipping by, most of them no longer under the control of their drivers. At 65 miles an hour in a soft-sprung comfort car, the operator was aiming, not driving.

"You embarrassed me in front of her."

"How?"

"By ordering me up front like a dog. You have no feeling for real people because you are not people. And in front of her."

"All white men are like that," said Mrs. Liu. "That's why they need running dogs like you to work for them."

"Shit," said Remo, summing up the situation.

He had lost two of the three cars following him by pulling off the roadway. But the last car still was on his tail. With one hand, Remo unwrapped the red cellophane covering from a pack of cough drops on the dashboard. He smoothed it out as best he could, then held it in front of his eyes, peering through it as he drove through the pre-dawn darkness.

He continued looking through the red filter for a full two minutes, as he began to push the car to its limits. Sixty-five. Seventy. Eighty. Ninety. As he came to the top of a rise with the pursuit car some 400 yards behind him, he saw what he was looking for. As soon as he cleared the rise, he turned off his lights and dropped the piece of red cellophane. His eyes, now functional in the dark, saw clearly the Boston exit, and without lights at 90 miles an hour, Remo whipped around the turn, then began slowing down without hitting the brake.

In his mirror, he could see the pursuit car—its driver blinded by darkness—plow ahead on the Thruway toward New York. Goodbye car number three.

"Barney Oldfield," Chiun said. "A regular Barney Oldfield. Did it ever occur to you that your life would be safer if you stopped and did combat, Mr. Barney Oldfield?"

"You can fasten your seat belt."

"I am my own seat belt. But that is because I can control my body the way civilized people are supposed to. Perhaps you should fasten your seat belt. Heh, heh."

"Reckless, inconsiderate driving," said Mrs. Liu. "Do you know that driving at these speeds consumes gasoline more rapidly than driving at lower speeds? Besides, I want to find my husband, wherever he is, not precede him to heaven."

"Shit," said Remo, and it was the last thing he said until they reached Boston. He wondered if he had been wise to shake the tail. But his mission called for finding General Liu, not endangering the general's wife. His followers would pick him up again, if they hadn't already, and he wanted the meeting on his terms, when his decisions would not be warped because of the danger to the girl.

Now, he was in Boston, it was just after noon, and it felt somewhat exhilarating to know that someone thought you were worth $70,000 to kill. But as he walked back to his hotel, a vague anger began to grow. Only $70,000?

A basketball player recently was sued for jumping a team, the team claiming he was worth $4 million. Four million for him and his life, and only $70,000 for Remo's death. Inside the hotel lobby, Remo felt concentration on him. It was not strong and his anger had almost dulled his senses. Collecting the extra room key, he noticed a scruffy woman in a black dress and hat reading a newspaper. But her eyes didn't move across the columns.

Maybe he should sell tickets? He thought momentarily of collecting fees from everyone following him, Chiun and the girl. Maybe go up to the woman and say, "Uh, look. We're the in thing this week. We're going to be at Fenway Park on Saturday and you can't tail us without a ticket that night. I recommend a good box seat so you can use a knife or even your hands if one of us should wander near the bullpen."

But Remo had been trained better than that. One never gave away the knowledge he was being tailed. One gives away nothing. As Chiun had said in the first weeks of training at Folcroft when Remo's wrists were still sore from the current of the electric chair:

"Fear is all right for you. But never induce it in your victim. Never exert your will on him. Never let him know you even exist. Give him nothing of you. Be like the strange wind that never blows."

It had sounded like any other of the many riddles Remo did not understand, and it took him years at his trade before he was able to perfect the skill of sensing people watching him. Some people experienced it occasionally, usually in crowded situations.

For Remo, it was everywhere, all the time. Like in the lobby of the Hotel Liberty. And the apparently harmless old lady putting the spot on Remo.

Remo strolled to the elevator. A crummy $70,000. The car stopped at the 11th floor. A basketball player worth four million dollars.

The car door closed behind him. As the elevator started up, he went up in full jump, his chest stretched out to catch the nine-foot ceiling. And down he came again, dribbling an imaginary basketball, with a small cry of victory.

He had seen Lew Alcindor in a game once, and on that jump, Remo would have gone over him. On most jumps, he would have, Remo thought. What Lew Alcindor did better than Remo was stand taller. And, of course, find a better job. One, not only with retirement benefits, but with retirement.

Remo wondered, when that last day came, if they would ever find a trace of his body. "That's the biz, sweetheart," he said to himself and unlocked the door to his room.

Chiun was sitting in the middle of the floor, his legs crossed, humming happily to himself, a tuneless, nameless song that he used to express happiness at a joyous event. Remo was immediately suspicious.

"Where's Mei Soong?" he asked.

Chiun looked up almost dreamily. He wore his white robes of joy, one of the fifteen changes he had brought with him. Remo had a valise, the girl brought everything in her coat pockets, and Chiun had a steamer trunk.

"She's fine," he said to Remo.

"Where is she fine?"

"In her bathroom."

"She's taking a shower?"

Chiun reverted to his humming.

"Is she taking a shower?"

"Ooowah, hummmmm, ooohwah . . . nee . . . shu . . . hmmmmmm."

"Chiun, what did you do with her?" Remo demanded.

"As you suggested, I made sure she would not escape."

"You bastard," Remo said, dashing through the adjoining door. He had rented three rooms, the central one being Mrs. Liu's. The bathroom door was locked from the outside.

Remo opened it. And saw her.

She hung from the shower curtain rod, trussed like an animal being brought back to a village for a feast. Her wrists were bound with strips torn from sheets, and tied together over the chrome shower rod. Her feet were bound in the same fashion, over the shower rod, and her body made a "u" as she faced the ceiling, her mouth gagged, her thick black hair flowing toward the floor, her clothes laying in a pile by the tub. She was nude.

Her eyes were red with anger and fear, and she looked pleadingly at Remo as he threw the door open.

Remo quickly untied her feet and gently placed them on the rim of the white bathtub, then untied her hands. When her hands were free, she went for his throat, trying to dig her nails into the flesh. But Remo caught the hands with his left, and untied her gag with his right.

"Hold on," he said.

She screamed something in Chinese.

"Now wait a minute. Let's talk," he said.

"Talk, you fascist beast? You tied me up."

"I did not."

"Your running dog did."

"He lost his head. He won't do that again."

"Do not take me for a child, beast. I know the tricks. Your partner abuses me. You are friendly and then convince me of the virtues of capitalism. You do this because you have killed General Liu and now you wish me to join your capitalist clique and make a false report to the People's Republic of China."

"This is no hustle," Remo said. "I'm sorry."

"The word of a capitalist. How can I trust anyone without social consciousness?"

"I'm not lying." Remo could see her body untense and set itself in quiet hostility to him. He released her wrists. She dropped her hands, and appeared to be going for her clothes, when she moved for a sneak punch, which Remo dodged without even moving his feet or changing his expression.

"Bastard," she said, angrier now because she had missed. "I am leaving this country now and heading back for Canada and then home. You may stop me by killing me as you did my husband. But my disappearance will be the final proof my government needs of your country's perfidy."

Remo watched her step into her coarse white panties of material that would be unsuitable for any American or Japanese woman.

The mission was now a failure. He had been taken out of normal function, assigned as a bodyguard to prevent what had just happened—or something worse—and now he watched Mei Soong prepare to leave, with Dr. Smith's and the President's peace melted in the heat of her anger.

Since he was out of function already, he would step further out of function. It was a crazy ballgame and if the pitcher were suddenly assigned to play first base, then, dammit, he would do it the way he thought best.

While Mei Soong was hitching on her bra from behind, Remo stepped close to her and unhooked it. She tried to break free by kicking backwards toward his groin, but Remo spun her around and, laughing carried her into the bedroom and went down with her onto the tan bedspread, pressing her into the mattress, as her arms flailed wildly at his head.

CHAPTER ELEVEN

In the other room, Chiun was amusing himself, reading a detailed analysis proving how little the New York Times understood of the turmoil inside China. The Page One article talked of militaristic elements anxious to stop the premier's visit to America and of the desire among China's "more stable leadership"—Chiun snorted at that—to solidify relations with the United States.

In Washington, the President was still planning for the Premier's trip, the Times said, but there were rumors that he was fearful the Chinese would cancel it.

Chiun put the paper down. The press was slowly beginning to learn of the disappearance of General Liu. That could be serious.

But cancel the trip? Not if the Chinese thought there was any way of milking even one dollar from the fools who ran the United States.

His attention was distracted by noise from inside Mei Soong's room, and he cocked an ear to listen.

Inside, Remo had pinned her knees with his body and with his left hand manacled her wrists together above her head. Her soft, smooth face was twisted now, the teeth clenched tight, the lips drawn thin, the eyes narrowed, a mask of pure hate. "Beast, beast, beast," she yelled and Remo smiled down at her to let her see his calm and to understand it, to know that his need did not make him weak and that he was in full control.

Her body would be his instrument. Her hate and violent struggle would be used to his ends, not hers, because in fighting, she had surrendered her control and all he had to do was exploit it.

His right hand moved beneath her smooth buttocks, and neatly tore the coarse cloth panties. With his fingers, he began to work the muscles of her buttocks, while he kept his face impassive. His hand worked to the small of her back, and then down again to the other cheek, reinforcing the tension of the lower body.

He entertained the thought to kiss her on the lips, but that would be wrong now. He was not doing this for fun. Chiun had taken even that away from him. He had done the impossible. He had made sex boring.

It was on an early training session, this one a month's long regimen at Plensikoff's Gymnasium in Norfolk, Va., a small building off Granby Street that only a handful of people knew was not an abandoned warehouse.

It had started with the lectures, the dry riddles and Remo asking, "Okay, when do I get laid?"

Chiun had talked about the orgasm, which was a major requirement for a relationship only when nothing else held it together. Chiun was sitting on the gymnasium floor in a robin's egg blue kimono with yellow birds sewn on.

"When do I get laid?" Remo asked again.

"I see we have exceeded your usual attention span of two minutes. Could it hold your attention if a naked woman were to walk in here?"

"It might," Remo said. "But she's got to have big jugs."

"The American mind," said Chiun. "You should be distilled and bottled as the American mind. Now. Imagine the woman standing here."

"I knew it was too good to be true," Remo said. The wooden gymnasium floor was hard and making his duff numb. He shifted his weight and saw Chiun cast a disapproving look at him. Afternoon sunlight came through the dust-lathered windows of the gymnasium and Remo could follow a fly in its light, until it disappeared between the windows, then reappeared again in light.

"Are you concentrating?"

"Yes," said Remo.

"You're lying," said Chiun.

"All right. All right. What do you want me to do?"

"See a woman standing naked before you. Create her outline. See her breasts. Her hips, the juncture of her legs. Do you see?"

Remo indulged the old man. "Yeah, I see her."

"You do," Chiun commanded.

Remo did.

"But you are looking wrong. What does her face look like?"

"I can't see her face."

"Ah, very good. You cannot see her face because that is the way you see women. Faceless. Now try to see her face. I will draw it for you. Simply. And I will tell you what she is feeling standing there undraped. What do you think she is feeling?"

"Cold."

"No. She is feeling exactly what she has been taught to feel since childhood. It could be embarrassment, or excitement, or fear. Maybe power. But her feelings about sex are social. And that is the key to awakening a woman's body. Through her social upbringing. You see, we must. . . ."

Remo counted two more flies in a dogfight. The overhead lights were one, but they were weak, doing little but shining out the information that they were there.

Then he felt the slap across the face.

"This is important," said the old man.

"Shit," said Remo, his cheek stinging. He stayed with the lecture as long as the cheek stung, which was approximately a half hour, and he learned how to unleash the woman's senses, the proper time, control of himself, and how to use his body as a weapon against hers.

The next time he had sex, the woman was ecstatic and Remo less than pleased. He tried again with someone else. This time, it was like an exercise for him, albeit delirious enjoyment for his partner. One more try convinced him that Chiun had managed to rob him of his enjoyment of sex, and to transform it into just another weapon.

And now, in a Boston hotel room, he was using that weapon to assault the mind and body of a young Chinese woman with small but exquisitely symmetrical young breasts.

He allowed her to writhe beneath him until perspiration formed on her forehead and her breath came quickly, and all the while, he kneaded the base of her spine. When Remo felt her warm, lush body give less to each movement, accepting the fact that he was irresistibly atop her, accepting at least his presence because she could not fight it, the presence of an imperialist Caucasian about to commit rape, a man she hated, he stopped massaging the base of her spine and her cheeks, and slowly moved his fingertips down her right thigh to her kneecap, very slowly so she would not think it a deliberate move.

She stared up at him resignedly, dull eyes and set mouth, saying nothing, but all her muscles finally alive and warmed from use.

He stared into her eyes, and let his right hand rest on the kneecap as though it would not move again, as if they would stay like this for day upon tedious day. She smelled of freshness, something beyond bottling, the healthy fresh aliveness of youth. Her skin was golden and soft, her face eggshell round and amooth, her eyes deep black. And then Remo saw it in the eyes, that small slight desire that his hand move up again across her thigh.

And he did so, but hesitantly, and even slower than before. But coming down to the knee again, he brought it down faster and slightly harder, then to the inside of the thigh, steady smooth warm strokes always stopping short of her essence. The dark rims capping her golden mounds formed sharper edges and Remo lowered his mouth to their concentric circles, then drew a tongue line down to her navel, while never ceasing the slow rhythmic force on the tender inner thigh.

He saw her mouth relax. She would allow herself to be taken, even though she did not like it. This is what she would be telling herself. But she was lying to herself. She wanted him.

Remo still held her small wrists above her head. He had broken the pattern of taking her by force. If he let go she would be obliged by her upbringing to try to fight her way free. So he held them. But easily.

With his right hand, he worked her breasts, then her navel, her upper arms, her inner thighs before finally reaching her moistened essence. She was moaning, "You white bastard. You white bastard."

Then, the penetration, but not fully, holding out, waiting for her to demand. And she demanded. "Damn you, I want it," she groaned, her dark eyes almost disappearing beneath her upper lids.

He released her wrists now and with both hands began kneading her buttocks again, increasing pressure, increasing penetration, bringing maximum pressure on her sensory organ, willing her into orgasm, holding only for a bare moment of peak, then relaxing to the usual, ho-hum, hysterical shrieks of the woman.

"Ah," yelled Mei Soong, her eyes shut in ecstasy, "Fuck Mao. Fuck Mao," and Remo suddenly withdrew fully and stood up. Under different circumstances, he would have stayed, but now he needed her to follow him, to be unsure that he would ever want her again. So he left her exhausted on the couch, and zipped up his trousers, having performed fully clothed.

And then he saw Chiun standing in the doorway, shaking his head.

"Mechanical," he said.

"What the hell do you want?" Remo said, angrily. "You give me 25 exact steps to follow and then you call it mechanical."

"There is always room for artistry."

"Why not show me how it's done?"

Chiun ignored him. "Besides, I think to do it in front of another person is disgusting. But you Americans and Chinese are pigs anyway."

"You're some piece of work," said Remo who had enjoyed less passion in his sex, than a man across the street intended to enjoy in Remo's death.

CHAPTER TWELVE

"I must talk to you, Chiun," said Remo. He shut the door behind him, leaving Mei Soong still sprawled, exhausted and drained, across her bed.

Chiun sat down on the gray carpeted floor, his legs crossed before him in the lotus position. His face was passive.

Remo sat down before him. He could, if he wished, sit for hours now, having worked for years on his concentration and body control He was taller than Chiun, but as they sat, their eyes were level.

"Chiun," said Remo. "You're going to have to return to Folcroft. I'm sorry, but you're just too much trouble."

And then Remo caught something, which he was sure he did not catch. He could not quite define it. Not in Chiun. In anyone else, he would have decided a preparation for attack or a decision to attack. But that was impossible in Chiun. For one, Remo knew Chiun had eliminated any telegraphing motions, at least as much as he was able, right down to the first flash of preparation which could sometimes be seen in the eyes but more often in the shift of the spinal column. Most people adept at the trade learned to give nothing from their eyes, but the shift in the spinal column was like hanging out a sign.

And Remo, if he did not know that Chiun did not give out signs, and if he did not know that Chiun had deep affection for him, would have sworn at that moment, in the hotel room in Boston, with the doors shut and the blinds drawn, that Chiun had just decided to kill him.

"Something troubles you," said Chiun.

"The truth is, Chiun, that you've become impossible.

You're going to blow this mission with your nonsense about the Chinese. I've never before seen you less than perfect, and now you're acting like a child."

"Smith has ordered you to send me back?"

"Now don't get upset. This is just a professional decision."

"What I am asking is did Smith order my return?"

"And if I told you he did, would it make things easier for you?"

"I must know."

"No. Smith did not order it. I want it."

Chiun raised his right hand delicately, signalling that he wished to make a point and that Remo should listen with care.

"I will explain to you, my son, why I do things you do not understand. To understand actions, one must understand the person. I must tell you of me and my people. And you will know why I do what I do, and why I hate the Chinese.

"Many people would think of me as an evil man, a professional killer of people, a man who teaches other people to kill. So be it. But I am not an evil man. I am a good man. I do what I am supposed to do. It is our way of life in Sinanju, a way we needed for survival.

"You come from a rich country. Even the poorest countries of the west are rich compared to my home. I have told you some small things about my village of Sinanju. It is poor as you do not understand poor. The land can support only one-third of the families who live there. That is in the good years.

"Before we discovered a way to survive, we would destroy half our girl babies at birth. We would drop them sadly into the bay, and say we were sending them home, to be reborn during better times. During famines, we would send the male children home the same way, waiting for another time more propitious to birth. I do not believe that by dropping them in the bay we send them home. And I do not believe that most of our people believe it.

But it is an easier thing for a mother to say than that she gave her child to the crabs and sharks. It is a lie to make grief more endurable.

"Imagine China as the body and Korea as the arm. In the armpit is Sinanju, and to that village the lords of China and the lords of Korea would exile people. Royal princes who had betrayed their fathers, wise men, magicians who had done evil. One day, I believe in your year of 400 and our day of the nightingales, a man came to our poor village.

"He was as no man we had ever seen. He looked very different. He was from the island beyond the peninsula. From Japan. He was before ninjutsu, before karate, before all. He was, on his own island, accursed, having taken his mother as a woman. But he was innocent. He did not know she was his mother. But they punished him nevertheless, taking out his eyes with bamboo sticks."

Chiun's voice began to quiver as he imitated pomposity: " 'We cast you to the scum of this scum land,' the Japanese captain told the poor blind man. 'Death is too good for you.' And the blind man answered."

Chiun's voice now exuded integrity. His eyes lifted to the ceiling.

" 'Hark,' the man said. 'You who have eyes, do not see. You, who have hearts, know not mercy. You, who have ears, do not hear the waves lap upon your boat. You, who have hands, do not comfort.

" 'Woe be to you, when your hardheartedness returns and no doves mark its trail in peace. Because I see now a new people of Sinanju. I see a people who will settle your petty disputes. I see men of men. I see people of goodness, bringing their wrath to your foolish squabbles. From this day forth, when you approach Sinanju, bring money for the wars you cannot fight. That is the tax I place upon you and upon all those not from this village. To pay for the services you cannot do yourself, because you know not piety.' "

Chiun obviously was very happy with the story.

"Now, my son," he said to Remo. "Tell me what you think of this tale. With truth."

Remo paused.

"The truth," Chiun said.

"I think it's the same as the kids going home. I think the people of Sinanju became professional assassins because they had no other way to make a living. I think the story is just another way of making a shit deal more acceptable."

Chiun's face narrowed, the normal wrinkles becoming canyons, his hazel eyes burning. His lips were evil thin lines. He hissed: "What? Is that the truth? Will you not reconsider?"

"If I am to lose your affection, little father, because I tell the truth, then I will lose it. I do not want a lie between us because what we have dies with a lie. I think your story of Sinanju is a myth, made up to explain reality."

Chiun's face relaxed, and he smiled. "I think so, too. Heh, heh. But you almost lied there because you did not wish to offend me. Heh, heh. It is a beautiful story, no?"

"It is beautiful."

"Well, back to business. In the year 1421, the Emperor Chu Ti hired our master, the man the village lives on."

"One man?" Remo asked.

"That is all that is needed. If the man is good enough, that is all that is needed to support the weak and the poor and the aged of the village, all those who cannot fend for themselves. And our master brought with him into China the sword of Sinanju, seven feet long and of the finest metal. It was his task to execute the architects and the builders of the T'ai-ho Tien, the throne room, because they had installed and knew the secret passageways."

Remo interrupted. "Why would he need a sword?"

"The hand is for attack. But the sword is for execution."

Remo nodded.

"He fulfilled his duties to the letter. On the afternoon of

the completion of the T'ai-ho Tien, the Emperor called all the architects and builders to the secret passageway, where he had said they would receive their reward.

"But he was not there to reward them. Only the master. Whaa, the sword moved right. Whaa, the sword moved left. Whaa, the sword moved down, and scarcely a man there saw the blade or knew what was happening. Whaa."

Chiun two-handed a large, imaginary sword. It had to be imaginary because no seven-foot sword could move that quickly with that little effort.

"Whaa. And he left the sword there with the bodies, to return for it after he was paid. But before he was paid, the Emperor invited him to dinner. But the master said, 'I can not. My people are hungry. I must return with their sustenance.' This is the truth I speak, Remo.

"And the Emperor gave the master a poisoned fruit. And the master was helpless."

"Don't you people have a defense against poison?"

"There is only one. Not eating. Know your food. That is your weakness too, my son. Although no one need try to poison you because you poison yourself daily. Pizza, hot dogs, roast beef, mashed potatoes, the skin of poultry. Pheewww. Anyway, the master awoke in a field, because of his great strength, only numbed. On foot, weak, and without his powers, he returned to Sinanju. By the time he arrived, they were again sending the newborn home."

Chiun's head dropped. He stared at the floor.

"For me to fail is to send the children home. I cannot do that, even if you were the assignment. For today, I am the master."

"That's your tough shit, Chiun, not mine." Remo's voice was cold.

"You are right. It is my tough shit."

"What about the architects and builders? Why did they deserve death?"

"That is the price one must expect to pay for working for the Chinese."

"And Sinanju paid that price also," Remo said. He was

98

beyond anger, in the whirlpool of frustration, unable to strike out at anything that would not hurt him more. He had always known that Chiun was professional and if need be Remo himself would be sacrificed. But he did not like to hear it.

"One always pays the price. Nothing is free," Chiun said. "You are paying it now. You are exposed, known, your greatest weapon, that of surprise, gone. You have no children whose lives depend on your service, no mothers to tell themselves lies because you failed. Your skills can give you the good life. Go. Escape."

The anguish Remo had felt left for a new pain, the hurt of telling a good friend something you did not tell even yourself. He leaned forward, hoping to avoid telling Chiun.

"What's the matter, Chiun? Don't you have it to kill me?"

"Do not be silly. Of course, I would kill you. Although death would be easier for me."

"I cannot abandon this assignment," Remo said.

"Why?"

"Because," Remo said, "I have children too. And they are being sent home, by heroin, by war, by crime, by people who think it a good thing to blow up buildings and shoot policemen and stretch the laws of our country until they protect no one. The children who are harmed by this are my children. And if we have a chance, that someday, we will not have wars, and our streets will be safe, and children are not poisoned by drugs and men robbed by other men, then, that day will I escape. Then, that day, will I put down my nation's sword. And until that day, I will do my job."

"You will do your job until you are killed."

"That's the biz, sweetheart."

"That's the biz," said Chiun.

And then they smiled, Chiun first, then Remo, because they felt that first little tinge that tells you someone is zoning in on you, and it would be good now to use their bodies again.

There was a knock on the door.

"Come in," said Remo, rising from the floor. It felt good to stretch his legs. The door opened, admitting the woman whom he had pointedly not noticed noticing him in the lobby. She was dressed now as a maid.

"Hello, sir," she said. "Your air conditioning is malfunctioning. We'll have to turn it off and open the window."

"By all means," Remo said sweetly.

The woman, giving more signals than the public address system at Grand Central Station, clopped into the room and pulled up the blinds. She did not look at either man, but was stiff and programmed and even perspiring.

Chiun made a face, indicating almost shock at the incompetence of the setup. Remo squelched a laugh.

The woman opened the window, and Chiun and Remo simultaneously spotted the sniper across the street, in a room one story higher than theirs. It was as easy as if the woman had shone a flashlight into the room across the street.

Remo grabbed her hands in his.

"Gee, I don't know how to thank you for this. I mean, it was getting stuffy in here."

"That's all right," said the woman, attempting to break free. Remo applied slight pressure behind her thumbs and stared into her eyes. She had been avoiding his, but could avoid them no longer.

"That's all right," she repeated. "I was glad to help." Her left foot began to tap nervously.

"I'd like to phone the desk and thank them for your help," Remo said.

"Oh, no. Don't do that. It's part of the service." The woman was so locked in her tension now that she had turned off her feelings, lest they explode. Remo let her go. She would not look back when she left the room, but would run where she must run.

Remo wanted them both, together. He did not want any corpses in his own room, or cluttering his hallway. But if he got them in their room, neat, done, then perhaps a small bite to eat. He had not eaten since the previous day.

She stumbled through the door, and it shut with a crack behind her and she was gone. Remo waited a moment, then said to Chiun:

"You know, I could go for seafood tonight."

"The sniper has been to Sinanju," said Chiun.

"Yeah, I thought so. You know, I felt him zoning in through the blinds." Remo held the doorknob.

"Incredibly effective," Chiun said, "except of course when it is incredibly ineffective. When the victim, not the shooter, is in control of the relationship. It was originally done with arrows, you know."

"You haven't taught me the firing yet."

"If you're alive in a few weeks, I will. I will keep him occupied," Chiun said, swaying slowly, as though dodging and teasing the end of a long, slow spear.

"Thanks," said Remo, opening the door.

"Wait," said Chiun.

"Yes?" said Remo.

"We had seafood yesterday."

"You can have vegetables. I'll have lobster."

"I'd like duck. Duck would be nice if cooked properly."

"I hate duck," Remo said.

"Learn to like it."

"See you later," said Remo.

"Think about duck," said Chiun.

CHAPTER THIRTEEN

Ricardo deEstrana y Montaldo y Ruiz Guerner was a dead man. He had placed his beloved weapon on the soft bed behind him, and sat in the chair by the window, September giving chill to his bones, Boston hooting noisily at him from below.

And he stared at the smiling Korean who now sat still in the lotus position in the room across the street. Guerner had seen blinds open, had felt the presence of his victims even before they were open, saw them, then began to create the link between the bullet and the skull of the target. At first, it seemed easier than easy, because the vibrations were there, that feeling between him and what he was shooting at, and it was stronger than ever before.

The target was talking to Maria, and then Maria left, but a strong feeling from the Korean overpowered that from his primary victim and demanded that the Korean be killed first. And so, Guerner sighted, touching the imaginary spear which was his rifle to the yellow forehead, but just missing, and reaching again, and not quite able to keep the spear there, unable to get the correct shot, just moving the barrel back and forth. And then it was only a rifle in his hands, and for years, ever since Sinanju, he had not used a rifle merely as a rifle. He had been in North Korea as a consultant, and he had visited that village, and been outshot by a child, and they had apologized that the master was not there to show him some real shooting, and for a ridiculously small sum of money, they had taught him the technique.

He had thought then that they were foolish. But now staring down the sights of his gun, he knew why the price was cheap. They had given him nothing, only a false confidence which would now be his death, now that he had met the master who had been missing that day years ago.

He tried to sight, like a normal shot, but the gun shook. He had not used it like that for years.

He concentrated on his bullet, the trajectory, blocking out the sight of the weaving Korean, and when all was set again, he put the imaginary spear to the victim's head, but the head was not there and Guerner's fingers trembled.

Shaking, he put the cold rifle on the bed. The elderly Korean, still in his lotus position, bowed, and smiled.

Guerner bowed his respects and folded his arms. His main target had disappeared from the room and would undoubtedly be at his door momentarily.

It had not been a bad life, although if he could have begun life with the vines, instead of entering this business, then perhaps it might have been better.

That was a lie, of course, he realized. He felt that he should pray now, but somehow it would not be right, and what did he really have to ask for. He had taken everything he wanted. He was satisfied with his life, he had planted his vines and harvested his grapes, so what more could he ask for.

So, Guerner silently addressed whatever deity might be out there and thanked the deity for the good things he had enjoyed. He crossed his legs, and then a request came to his mind.

"Lord, if you are there, grant me this. That there be no heaven and there be no hell. Just that it be all over."

The door opened and Maria entered puffing. Guerner did not turn around.

"You get him?" she asked.

"No," said Guerner.

"Why not?" asked Maria.

"Because he's going to get us. That's one of the risks of the business."

"What the hell are you talking about?"

"We lose, Maria."

"But it's only 50 yards."

"It could be the moon, my dear. The rifle's on the bed. Feel free to use it."

Guerner heard the door shut. "No need to shut the door, my dear. Doors won't stop these people."

Maria said, "I didn't shut the . . ." and then Guerner heard the crack of bone and a body bouncing onto the bed, then clumping into the wall near him. He looked to his left. Maria, her hair still scraggly, now was soaked with dark blood oozing from her broken skull. She could not have felt a thing, probably had not even seen the hands that performed the execution. Even in death, she looked so incredibly unkempt.

Guerner had another request of God, and asked that Maria be judged by her intentions, not her deeds.

"Hi there, fella, how's the sniper business?" came the voice from behind.

"Fine until you messed it up."

"That's the biz, sweetheart."

"If you don't mind, would you stop the small talk and get it over with?"

"Well, you don't have to be snotty about it."

"It's not that. It's just that I'm tired of dealing with peasants. Now, please, do what you must do."

"If you don't like dealing with peasants, why didn't you become a court chamberlain, shmuck?"

"I believe the job market was depressed at the time," Guerner said, still not turning toward the voice.

"First a couple of questions. Who hired you?"

"She did. The corpse."

"Who'd she work for?"

"Some Communist group or other. I'm not sure which."

"You can do better."

"Not really."

"Try."

"I did."

"Try harder."

Guerner felt a hand on his shoulder and then a vise, crushing nerve and bone, and incredible pain where his right side was and he groaned.

"Try harder."

"Aaaah. That's all I know. There's $70,000 in her purse."

"Okay. I believe you. Say, how's the roast duck in this town?"

"What?" said Guerner, starting to turn, but never finishing. Just a flash. Then nothing.

CHAPTER FOURTEEN

Remo drove off the New York Thruway on the same route General Liu's car had taken. It was a typical modern American highway junction with a confusion of signs stretched like meaningless miniature billboards 25 feet above the highway, so that to find a particular sign, one had to read them all.

It was a tribute to the thoughtlessness of highway planners that if Remo had not been the recipient of extensive training in mind and body control, he would have missed the turnoff.

The noon traffic seemed alive on the sunny fall day, perhaps a pre-lunch rush or just the normal clogging of an artery feeding a major city of the world.

Chiun had been making small, gasping sounds since the New York City air, a fume-laden, lung-corroding poison, had first seeped into the car's air conditioning.

"Slow death," Chiun said.

"Because of the insensitivity of the exploitative ruling class to the people's welfare. In China, we would not allow air like this."

"In China," Chiun said, "people do not have cars. They eat excrement."

"You allow your slave much freedom," Mei Soong said to Remo. The trio sat in the front seat, Mei Soong between the two men, and Chiun pressed as far against the passenger's door as he could get. Remo had not bothered to switch cars, and frankly hoped he was being followed. Time was getting short in the search for General Liu and he wanted contact made as soon as possible.

Remo did not like Chiun sitting near the window in his

106

present mood, although for most of the trip Remo had been careful to avoid cars with peace emblems. Remo had been concentrating on Liu's disappearance, hoping for a flash of inspiration.

Then he had heard Chiun humming happily, and snapped to full consciousness, looking around carefully. Nothing wrong. Then he saw what unleashed the joy in Chiun's heart. A small foreign car with a peace emblem was passing on their right.

As the car moved by, Chiun, staring straight ahead, shot an arm through the open window, flicking at something. Remo caught sight of it in the rearview mirror. A clinketing sideview mirror going back up the road, shattering in shards of glass, bouncing as it disappeared out of sight.

It had happened so fast, of course, the driver of the other car never saw Chiun's wraithlike hand snap out, picking off the mirror. Up ahead, Remo had seen the driver look around in a little confusion and shake his head. Chiun hummed even louder, in joyous contentment.

So Remo had watched for the peace banner cars all the way back to New York. Once, he had tried to foil Chiun. He came close while passing a car with a peace sign, then turned away at the last moment, seeing how close he could come to fooling Chiun.

Remo wound up with a sideview mirror in his lap. Chiun loved that, especially when it bounced off Remo and landed on Mei Soong's hands.

"Heh, heh," Chiun had said, his victory complete.

"Bet you feel proud of yourself," Remo had said.

"Only feel proud when you defeat worthy opponent. Not proud at all. Heh, heh. Not proud at all."

This putdown had lasted Chiun all the way to the turnoff in New York City, with only an occasional "heh, heh, not proud at all."

Remo followed the route he knew General Liu had taken. Under the Jerome Avenue elevated train he drove, past the Mosholu Golf Course, to a crowded business

107

district, shaded in the sunlight of day by the black grimy elevated traintracks, darkening the whole street. Hardware shops, delicatessens, supermarkets, more restaurants, two dry cleaners, laundries, candy and toy stores. Then Remo turned off the avenue two blocks beyond where General Liu had disappeared and prowled the neighborhood with the car. They were clean neat buildings, six stories high at the most, all brick, and all surprisingly quiet for New York City.

Yet Remo knew that New York City was not really one city but a geographical conglomeration of thousands of provincial neighborhoods, each as far away spiritually from the glamor of New York City as Sante Fe, New Mexico.

These neighborhoods—and sometimes just one apartment building consituted a neighborhood—enjoyed their own ethnic composition, Italian, Irish, Jewish, Polish; proof that the melting pot didn't really melt anything, but instead allowed the unmixed particles to go floating around happily in a common stew.

The houses on both sides of Jerome Avenue, between the Grand Concourse, the main thoroughfare of the Bronx, and the beginning of the elevated train, were the same. Neat, none more than six stories. All brick. Yet there were small differences.

"Chiun," Remo said, "do you know what I'm looking for?"

"Not sure."

"Do you see what I see?" Remo asked.

"No."

"What do you think?"

"This is an outskirt of a larger city."

"Notice anything different from one block to another?"

"No. This is one place all over the place. Heh, heh." Chiun knew when he created a phrase in English and would punctuate it with a laugh that was not a laugh.

"We'll see," Remo said.

Mei Soong piped up. "It is obvious that the middle level

of your rulers lives here. Your secret police and army. Your nuclear bomber pilots."

"The lower proletariat," Remo said.

"A lie," she insisted. "I do not believe the masses live in buildings like these with street lights on corners and shops nearby under that train in the air."

Remo parked the car in front of a brown brick building with a tudor entrance and two rows of green hedges cut very thin, bordering the steps that led to the entrance. "Wait here," he told Mei Soong and motioned Chiun to follow.

"I'm pretty sure I know how General Liu disappeared," Remo whispered to Chiun as they walked away from the car.

"Who do you think you are, Charley Chan?" asked Chiun. "You are not trained in this sort of thing."

"Quiet," Remo said. "I want you to observe."

"Right on, Sherlock, heh, heh."

"Where'd you pick that up?"

"I watch television at Folcroft."

"Oh, I didn't know they had TV there."

"Yes," said Chiun. "My favorite shows are *Edge of Night* and *As the World Turns*. They are so beautiful and lovely."

On Jerome Avenue, it became clear to Chiun also. As they strolled through the busy shopping district, they drew curious glances from passersby, the fruit peddler, students with DeWitt Clinton High School jackets, a policeman collecting his weekly tithe from a bookie.

They stopped in front of a lot clustered with unmarked gravestones, and an incredibly ornate white marble angel, undoubtedly ordered by a family that had come to its senses too late after the first shock of loss.

The fresh smell of grass from the municipal golf course came as a blessed gift, telling them that grass was alive and well and living in some sections of New York City.

The afternoon heat, surprising for September, bore down heavily on the now gummy asphalt.

A train clattered overhead spraying metal sparks where its wheels met the tracks.

"Chiun, General Liu never left Jerome Avenue at this point. There were no reports on his being seen, but in this neighborhood there's no way that a couple of men, one of them an Oriental in uniform, could just walk away. He must have been plopped into another car a couple of blocks from here and taken somewhere."

Remo scanned the street. "And you don't make any turnoff up there," he said, nodding north, "without meaning to. Not from a caravan of cars. His driver must have turned off, General Liu realized it and shot him. And perhaps the other man too. But whoever they were working with got the general before the rest of the caravan could catch up."

"Maybe he forced his driver to turn off," Chiun said.

"No, he wouldn't have to. They were his own men. He's a general, you know."

"And you know as much about Chinese internal politics as a roach knows about nuclear engineering."

"I know a general's man is a general's man."

"Do you also know why a general in an armored car can shoot two of his own men, and then not fire a shot at somebody who forces him from the car?"

"Maybe it all happened too fast. Anyway, Chiun. . . ." Remo stopped. "I've got it. That train overhead, you know where it goes? To Chinatown! That's it. They herded him on a train to Chinatown."

"Did no one notice the gang of men boarding the train? Did no one think it was odd to see a Chinese general struggling on a subway?"

Remo shrugged. "Just details."

"Everything seems clear to you because you do not know what you are doing, my son," said Chiun. "Perhaps General Liu is already dead."

"I don't think so. Why the big effort then to kill us?"

"A diversion."

Remo smiled. "Then they better up the price."

"They will," Chiun said. "Particularly now when the world learns that you are also a famous all-knowing detective."

"No more of your snot," Remo said. "You're just jealous because I figured it out and you couldn't. We're going to Chinatown. And find General Liu."

Chiun bowed from the waist. "As you desire, most worthy number one son."

CHAPTER FIFTEEN

There was trouble in China. More rumors of Mao's death. Newsmen pontificating on the inner struggles in Peking. All of them pontificating, and none of them knowing that a Chinese war faction was spreading the word that America intended to sabotage the peace talks by murdering emissaries. After all, if they could put men on the moon, could they not protect emissaries.?

So the reasoning went in China. So the whispers were whispered. And so, in a nation, where important decisions were discovered only after they had been implemented, people began to move before peace happened.

Remo commented on this, in a taxicab on his way to Chinatown. He had left his rented car at the midtown hotel they had checked into and had hailed a cab.

He was sure the answer was in Chinatown. He was sure General Liu's disappearance had something to do with the China turmoil. But he was no longer so confident of finding him. A needle in a haystack and only four days left before the Chinese cancelled the Premier's trip.

Remo was sure the Premier should, for safety sake, come to America now, without arrangements. A sudden trip announced only as he was in flight.

"Thank you, Mister Secretary of State," said Chiun.

"Do you think that the people of China will stand for one of their own beloved generals rotting in an American dungeon?" Mei Soong asked.

"The people in American prisons live better than you rice planters," commented Chiun to Mei Soong.

The cab driver knocked on the window. "This is it," he said.

Remo looked around. The streets were lit with merry lights and vendors sold pizza and hot sausages and little Italian pastries.

"This is Chinatown?" Remo asked.

"San Gennaro Festival. Little Italy spreads out during it."

Remo shrugged and paid the driver what seemed to be an excessive fare. He said nothing but he was disgusted. How was he going to find anyone—or be found—in this horde of Italians?

Now he pressed his way grimly down the middle of the street, squinting to close out the brightness of the overhead strings of lights. Mei Soong followed him, tossing insults back over her shoulder at Chiun, who shouted back at her. Their noise was deafening to Remo, not that anyone should have noticed. Hastily-erected plywood booths cluttering the already narrow streets drew crowds of Italians and the Oriental obscenities Chiun and Mei Soong shouted at each other sounded, in the din, only like warm greetings being exchanged by long-lost cousins from Castellamare.

None should have noticed the two shouting Orientals, but someone had. A young Chinese man, with long shiny hair, was ahead of them, leaning on the pole holding up the awning of an Italian zeppole booth, openly staring at them. He wore an olive drab Army-type jacket with a red star on each shoulder and a Mao-style fatigue hat, from under which hung a mass of long, sleek hair.

It was the third time they had passed him in the two-block festival stretch of Pell Street. He waited until all three had passed him and then Remo heard him shout. "Wah Ching."

"Wah Ching."

The cry echoed down the street, then was picked up by more voices, and shouted back. "Wah Ching. Wah Ching. Wah Ching."

Remo slowed his pace and Mei Soong stalked roughly ahead, as Chiun came up alongside him.

113

"What does that mean?" Remo asked.

"What?"

"Whatever they're yelling."

"They shout Wah Ching. It means China Youth," Chiun said.

They had walked through the festival area and the street ahead of them turned abruptly dark. And then Remo saw step out of an alley 40 yards ahead of them, four more young men. They wore the same costume as the man who had been trailing them, red-starred field jackets and fatigue caps.

They began to walk toward Remo, Chiun and Mei Soong, and Remo could sense the first youth drawing up on them from behind.

He took Mei Soong by the arm, and quickly but smoothly steered her around a corner into a narrow sidestreet. The street was brightly lighted but silent. Only the hum of airconditioners on the buff-colored three-story brick buildings that bordered the narrow street broke the silence, and the buildings served as a wall to seal out the shouting of the Italian hordes only a block away.

It had gone better than Remo had hoped. Perhaps they were going to find the fortune cookie among all that fettucini. But he had to keep the girl out of danger.

They stepped up onto the sidewalk and followed the twisting street, around the curve, when Remo drew up short. The street ended 100 feet ahead, passing through an unlit alley into the Bowery. Behind them, he heard footsteps approaching.

He pulled Mei Soong up short. "Come on," he said, "we're going to eat."

"Do you or the running dog have money? I have none."

"We'll bill it to the People's Rupublic."

The girl had still noticed nothing. She was used to being pulled around by Remo. Chiun, of course, would telegraph nothing, and Remo hoped that he had not, himself, given away their awareness that they were being followed.

As they walked casually, up the stairs to the Imperial Garden restaurant, Remo said to the girl: "When the revolution comes and your gang takes over, pass a law putting all your restaurants at street level. Around here, you're always walking up a flight or down a flight. It's like a city under a city."

"The exercise is good for the digestion," she said. Chiun snorted, but said nothing.

The restaurant was empty, and the waiter was sitting in the back at a booth in the back, going over the racing form. Without waiting, Remo walked to a booth midway down the row on the left side. He slid Mei Soong into a seat, then motioned Chiun in alongside her. He squeezed in on the opposite side of the gray formica table. By turning his body sideways, he could watch both the front door and the doors leading to the kitchen in the rear of the restaurant.

Chiun was smiling.

"What's so funny?"

"A rare treat. A Chinese restaurant. Have you ever been starved to death in seven courses? But of course a people with no honor have no real need of sustenance."

Mei Soong's answer was cut short by the appearance of the waiter, at their side.

"Good evening," he said in precise English. "We have no liquor."

"That's all right," Remo said. "We've come to eat."

"Very good, sir," he said, nodding to Remo. He nodded also to Mei Soong, and turned his head slightly to acknowledge Chiun. Remo could see Chiun's eyes look up into the waiter's face, evaporating the smile that was there. The waiter turned back to Mei Soong and exploded in a babble of Chinese.

Mei Soong answered him softly. The waiter babbled something, but before Mei Soong could answer, Chiun interrupted their melodic dialogue. In a parody of their Chinese sing-song, he spoke to the waiter, whose face

115

flushed, and he turned and walked rapidly to the kitchen in the rear.

Remo watched him push through the swinging doors, then turned to Chiun who was chuckling under his breath, wearing a smirk of self-satisfaction.

"What was that all about?" Remo asked.

Chiun said, "He asked this trollop what she was doing with a pig of a Korean."

"What did she say?"

"She said we were forcing her into a life of prostitution."

"What did he say?"

"He offered to call the police."

"What did you say?"

"Only the truth."

"Which is?"

"That no Chinese woman has to be forced into a life of prostitution. It comes naturally to them. Like stealing toilet paper. I told him too we would eat only vegetables, and he could return the dead cats to the icebox and sell them for pork tomorrow night. That seemed to upset him and he left. Some people cannot face up to the truth."

"Well, I'm just glad you handled it so pleasantly."

Chiun nodded an acknowledgement and folded his hands in front of him in an attitude of prayer, serene in the knowledge that no untrue or unkind word had passed his lips.

Remo watched the front door over Mei Soong's shoulder as he spoke to her. "Now remember. Keep your eyes open for any signal, anything that looks suspicious. If we're right, the people who have the general are around here somewhere, and they might like to add you to their collection. It gives us a chance of finding him. Maybe just a small chance. But a chance."

"Chairman Mao. He who does not look will not find."

"I was brought up believing that," Remo said.

She smiled, a small warm smile. "You must be careful,

116

capitalist. The seeds of revolution may lie in you ready to sprout forth."

She reached forward with her leg, and touched her knee to Remo's under the table. He could feel her trembling. Since the hotel room in Boston, she had studiedly spent her time, signaling Remo with touches and rubbing. But Remo had reacted coldly to them. She had to be kept close and obedient, and the best way was to keep her waiting.

By the flicker of distaste in Chiun's eyes, Remo could tell the waiter was returning. Remo watched him in a mirror over the entrance way, walking angrily back down the floor toward them, three dinner plates extended up his arm.

He stopped alongside the table, and placed one in front of Remo. "For you, sir."

He placed the second in front of Mei Soong. "And for the lovely lady."

He dropped the third one on the table in front of Chiun, and it splashed small drops on the table top.

"If we were to return in one year," Chiun said, "these drippings would still be here. Chinese, you know, never wash tables. They wait for earthquake or flood to jar dirt loose. It is the same with their bodies."

The waiter walked away, back toward the kitchen.

Mei Soong squeezed Remo's leg between both of hers under the table. As women always do in such situations to disclaim ownership of the brazen legs, she began to chatter incongruously.

"It looks good," she said. "I wonder if it is Cantonese or Mandarin."

Chiun sniffed the plate containing the usual jellied mass of colorless vegetables. "Mandarin," he said, "because it smells like dog. Cantonese smells like bird droppings."

"A people who would eat raw fish should not cavil at civilization," she said, spooning vegetables into her mouth.

"Is it civilized to eat birds' nests?"

And they were off again.

But Remo paid no attention to them. In the overhead mirror, he could see back through the round door windows into the kitchen where the waiter stood, talking to the young man who had spotted them on the street. The man was gesturing, and as Remo watched, he snapped his fatigue cap off his head and slapped it across the waiter's face.

The waiter nodded and almost ran back through the swinging doors. As he passed their table, he mumbled under his breath.

"What did he say?" Remo asked Chiun.

Chiun was still playing with his spoon in the vegetables. "He called me pig."

As Remo watched, the waiter picked up the phone in front and dialed. Just three digits. A long one and two shorts. It was the emergency number of the New York City police.

But why the cops? Unless he had been told to try to separate the girl from Remo and Chiun? What better way than to have the police grab them and spirit the girl off in the shuffle? Remo couldn't hear the waiter's words whispered into the phone, but he leaned over and whispered to Chiun. "We're going to have to split up. You get the girl back to the hotel. Make sure you're not followed. Stay with her. No calls, no visitors and don't open the door for anyone but me."

Chiun nodded.

"Come on, we're going," Remo said to the girl, disengaging his leg from between hers.

"But I haven't finished."

"We'll get a dragon bag to take it home." The police might be helpful. It might set it up so that any contact with the girl would have to come through Remo.

They walked to the front counter, where the waiter was just hanging up the phone.

"But you haven't had your tea?" he said.

"We're not thirsty."

"But your cookies?"

Remo leaned across the counter and grabbed his arm, above the elbow. "You want to hear your fortune? If you try to stop us from going out that door, you'll have a busted rib. Can your inscrutable mind fathom that?"

He reached into his pocket and tossed a ten dollar bill onto the glass counter. "Keep the change."

Remo led the way down the flight of stone stairs into the street. At their appearance, the five men in the field jackets, who had been lounging against the building across the street, started to walk toward them.

At the bottom of the stairs, Remo told Chiun, "You can go through that alley at the end of the street and grab a cab. I'll catch up to you later."

Remo stepped off the curb into the street, as Chiun took Mei Soong roughly by the arm and started walking off to the right, toward the Bowery. Remo had only to cover him long enough for him to reach the alley. There was no way anyone could catch up to Chiun in darkness, even with the girl as excess baggage.

Just then, the waiter stepped onto the top step and shouted, "Stop, thief!" The five men looked up at him, momentarily. Remo looked over his shoulder to his right. Chiun and the girl were gone. Vanished. As if the earth had opened and swallowed them.

The five young Chinese also saw that their target had vanished. They looked up and down the street, then dumbly at each other, then as if to take out their rage on something, they charged Remo.

Remo was careful not to hurt them. When the police arrived, he did not want the street cluttered with bodies. Too many complications. So he just moved in among them, dodging their punches and kicks. The waiter was still screaming at the top of the stairs.

Just then, a prowl car turned onto the narrow street. Its whirling red lamp shot slices of light along the buildings on either side of the street. The young Chinese saw it, and

119

they took to their heels, toward the end of the street and the narrow alley where a car could not follow them.

The police car pulled up alongside Remo and stopped with a squeal of tires on the cobblestone street.

As the two policemen jumped out onto the street, the waiter shouted to them: "That's him. Hold him. Don't let him get away."

The two policemen stood alongside Remo. "What's it all about, mac?" one of them said. Remo looked at him. He was young and blond and still a little frightened. Remo knew the feeling; he had experienced it in those early days on the force. Back when he was alive.

"Damned if I know. I came out of the restaurant and five thugs jumped me. And now he's yelling like a lunatic."

The waiter had walked up alongside the three of them now, still careful to keep back from Remo. "He hit me," he said, "and ran off without paying the bill. Those young men heard me yelling and tried to stop him. I want to press charges."

"I guess we'll have to take you in," the second policeman said. He was older, a veteran with patches of gray hair at the temples under his cap.

Remo shrugged. The waiter smiled.

The older policeman steered Remo into the back seat of the squad car, while the younger officer helped the waiter close up.

They returned to the car and slid into the front seat, while the older cop sat in beside Remo. Remo noticed that he sat with his gun side away from Remo. Standard procedure, but it was good to know that there were still some professional policemen around.

The precinct house was only a few blocks away. Remo was marched in between the two policemen and stood in front of the long oak desk, reminiscent of all those he had stood in front of himself with prisoners in tow.

"Assault case, Sergeant," the older patrolman said to the baldheaded officer behind the desk. "We didn't see it.

Do you have one of the squad around to handle it? We want to get back before that festival breaks up."

"Give them to Johnson in back. He's free," the sergeant said.

Remo wanted to hang around long enough to make sure the police had a record of his address. So he could be traced. Long ago, he had been given two authorized ways of dealing with an arrest.

He could do whatever physical had to be done. Of course, that was out of the question, since he was willingly going to leave his name and address, and he didn't need 30,000 cops looking for him at his hotel.

Or, the other way, he was allowed one phone call. He could call the number in Jersey City.

CHAPTER SIXTEEN

Jean Boffer Esq., 34 years old and a millionaire twice over, sat on the brown plush sofa in his penthouse living room, looking across the 71 square yards of lime green carpeting that had been laid that afternoon.

He had taken off his purple knit jacket and carefully removed from its inside pocket the little electronic beeper that was to signal him whenever his private telephone line was ringing.

He had worn the beeper for seven years, and it had yet to beep.

But he was a millionaire twice over because he was willing to wear it all the time, and because, if the private telephone line ever rang, he would be ready to do whatever had to be done. Without knowing it, he was the private, personal counsel to a professional assassin.

Just then, as he held the beeper in his hand, it went off, and he realized that in seven years he had never heard the sound it would make. It was a staccato, high-pitched squeak, but it was muffled at that moment by the bell of his private telephone line which was also ringing.

He reached over, carefully, not quite knowing what to expect and picked up the white telephone without a dial. The beeper went silent.

"Hello," he said, "Boffer."

"You're a good lawyer, I hear," said a voice which was supposed to say "You're a good lawyer, I hear."

"Yes. I think the best," which was what Jean Boffer Esq. had been told to say.

Boffer sat up smartly on the couch and placed the book of forensic medicine carefully on his coffee table.

"What can I do for you?" he said casually.

"I've been arrested. Can you spring me?"

"Is there any bail set?"

"If I wanted to get out on bail, I'd pay it myself. What can you do about getting the whole thing dropped?"

"Tell me what happened."

"I was set up. A restaurant in Chinatown. The owner says I assaulted him but he's full of crap. I'm being booked now."

"What restaurant? Is the owner still there?"

"Yeah, he's here. His name's Wo Fat. The restaurant's the Imperial Garden on Doyers Street."

"Keep the owner there until I get there. Diddle around. Tell the cops you want to press counter-charges. I'll be there in 20 minutes." He paused. "By the way, what's your name?"

"My name is Remo."

They hung up simultaneously. Boffer looked over at his wife who was wearing large pilot earphones, listening to a private stereo concern and putting polish on her fingernails. He waved at her and she pulled off the earphones.

"Come on, we're going to get something to eat."

"What can I wear?" She was wearing a white pants suit with gold brocade trim. It would have been appropriate for the captain's dinner on a Bahama cruise.

"We'll stop and buy you a field jacket. Come on, let's go."

His car was waiting downstairs, and he slid behind the driver's wheel, and tooled the expensive car north on Kennedy Boulevard to the Holland Tunnel approach. They were in the tunnel before either of them spoke.

"It's a case, isn't it?" his wife said, easing imaginary wrinkles from the front of her white pants suit.

"Just an assault. But I thought it was an excuse for a meal."

He pulled out of the tunnel, smiling to himself as he always did when he saw the Port Authority's incredible overhead sign which looked like a bowl of spaghetti run amok.

He eased his car into Chinatown, its streets dark and empty now, littered with zeppole shreds and crusts of pizza.

He stopped in front of the darkened Imperial Gardens Restaurant.

"But this place is closed," his wife said.

"Just a minute." He walked up the steps to the second floor entrance of the Imperial Gardens. The restaurant was darkened with only the faint glow from a 7½ watt nightlight shining in the rear of the main dining area. He peered in through the glass, noting in the glow the location of the tables around the kitchen door.

With his left hand, he felt up the side of the door, trying to find the external casing of the hinges. There was none.

He went back down the steps, three at a time, and reentered the car. "We'll eat in 15 minutes," he said to his wife, who was refreshing her lipstick.

The police precinct was only three blocks away, and he left his wife in the car as he went inside and walked up to the sergeant behind the 30-foot long oak desk.

"I've got a client here," he said. "Remo something."

"Oh yeah. He's in the detective's room. Him and some Chinaman are screaming at each other. Go right in, and look for Detective Johnson." He waved toward a room at the end of the large open room.

He walked in through the swinging wood door gate, to the open door. Inside he saw three men: one a Chinese; one sitting at the typewriter laboriously pecking out a report with two fingers was obviously Detective Johnson. The third man sat in the hard wooden chair, leaning back against a file cabinet.

Through the doorway, Boffer could see the skin slightly paler and tighter over his cheekbones, the mark of plastic surgery. The man's deep brown eyes looked up and burned into Boffer's for a moment. The eyes tipped off on everyone. But not on his new client. His eyes were deep brown and cold, as emotionless as his face.

Boffer rapped on the open frame of the door. The three men looked at him.

He stepped inside. "Detective Johnson, I'm this man's attorney. Can you fill me in?"

The detective came to the door. "Come on in, counsellor," he said, obviously amused by the striped purple suit. "Don't know why you're here? Nothing much to it. Wo Fat here says your client assaulted him. Your client is filing counter charges. They'll both have to wait until arraignment in the morning."

"If I could talk to Mr. Wo Fat for a minute, maybe I could clear the whole thing up. It's more of a misunderstanding than a criminal thing."

"Sure, go ahead. Wo Fat. This man wants to talk to you. He's a lawyer."

Wo Fat rose and Boffer took his elbow and steered him to the back of the room. He shook his hand.

"You run a fine restaurant, Mr. Fat."

"I've been in business too long to allow myself to be assaulted."

Boffer ignored him. "It's a shame we're going to have to close you down."

"What do you mean, close down?"

"There are very serious violations at your establishment, sir. The exterior doors, for instance, open inward. Very dangerous in the event of a fire. And very unlawful."

Wo Fat looked confused.

"And then of course, there's the seating plan. All those tables near the kitchen doors. Another violation. I know you run a fine establishment, sir, but in the interests of the public, my client and I will have to go into court with a formal complaint and bring about your closing as a health menace."

"Now, we should not be hasty," he said in his oiliest style.

"Yes, we should. We should withdraw the charges against my client immediately."

"He assaulted me."

"Yes sir, he probably did. In outrage at being caught in a restaurant which is an outright fire trap. It'll be a very interesting case. The publicity from the papers might hurt your business for a while, but I'm sure it will blow over. As will the stories about your assaulting a customer."

Wo Fat turned his hands up. "Whatever you want."

Detective Johnson had just reentered the room carrying two blue sheets used for booking.

"You won't need those, Detective," Boffer said. "Mr. Fat has decided to drop charges. It was just bad temper on both sides. And my client will drop them too."

"Suits me," the detective said. "Less paper work."

Remo had stood up and already had taken a few steps toward the door, in a smooth glide.

Boffer turned to Wo Fat. "That's correct, isn't it, sir?"

"Yes."

"And I've made no threats against you or any offers to induce you to take this action." He whispered, "Say no."

"No."

Boffer turned to the detective again. "And of course I stipulate the same for my client. Will that do?"

"Sure thing. Everyone can go."

Boffer turned to the door. Remo had gone. He was not outside in the main room of the precinct.

Out in front, his wife had her window rolled down. "Who was that lunatic?" she said.

"What lunatic?"

"Some man just ran out. He stuck his head in and kissed me. And said something stupid. And messed my lipstick."

"What did he say?"

"That's the biz, sweetheart. That's what he said."

CHAPTER SEVENTEEN

Remo was not followed back to the hotel. When he went into his room, Chiun was sitting on a sofa, watching a late night talk show host who was trying to probe the hidden significance of a woman with a face like a footprint, who had raised yelling and shouting to an art form.

"Where's Mei Soong?" Remo asked.

Chiun pointed over his shoulder toward her room.

"Anybody follow you?"

"No."

"By the way, how'd you do that down at the restaurant? Disappear, I mean?"

Chiun smirked. "If I tell you, then you will go tell all your friends, and soon everyone will be able to do it."

"I'll ask the girl," Remo said, walking toward her room.

Chiun shrugged. "We ran up a flight of stairs and hid in a doorway. No one thought of looking up."

Remo snorted. "Big deal. Magic. Hah."

He walked into the next room and Mei Soong purred at him. She walked toward him, wearing only a thin dressing gown.

"Your Chinatown is very nice. We must go back."

"Sure, sure. Anything you want. Has anyone tried to contact you since you got back here?"

"Ask your running dog. He allows me no freedom or no privacy. Can we go back to Chinatown tomorrow? I have heard that there is a marvelous school of karate that no visitor should miss."

"Sure, sure," Remo said. "Someone should try to contact you again. They'll probably be able to lead us to the general, so make sure I handle it."

"Of course."

Remo turned to go and she ran around to stand in front of him.

"You are angry? You do not like what you see?" She held her arms out and proudly thrust forth her young breasts.

"Some other time, kid."

"You look troubled. What are you thinking?"

"Mei Soong, I'm thinking that you are making it difficult for me to leave now," Remo said. Which was not what he was thinking. What he was thinking was that she had already been contacted because there was a new copy of Mao's Red Book on the end table near her bed, and she had not had a chance to buy one herself. Someone must have smuggled it to her. And suddenly, she was interested in going back to Chinatown, and seeing that wonderful karate school.

He said, "Let us sleep now, so we can go to Chinatown very early and look for the general."

"I am sure that tomorrow you will find him," she said happily, and threw her arms around Remo, burying her face against his chest.

Remo spent the night dozing in a chair against the door to her room, alert enough to detect any attempt by Mei Soong to leave. In the morning, he woke her roughly and said:

"Come on, we're going to buy you some clothes. You can't walk round this country in that damned greatcoat."

"It is a product of the People's Republic of China. It is a wellmade greatcoat."

"But your beauty should not be hidden under it. You are depriving the masses of the sight of the new healthy China."

"Do you really think so?"

"Yes."

"But I do not wish to wear goods produced from the

exploitation of suffering workers. The stitches made of their blood. The fabric made of their sweat. The buttons of their bones."

"Well, just some inexpensive clothes. A few garments. We're already too obvious to people as it is."

"All right. But just a few." Mei Soong held up a finger in lecture. "I will not profit from the capitalistic exploitation of slave labor."

"Okay," said Remo.

At Lord and Taylor's, Mei Soong discovered that Pucci workers were well paid. She adhered largely to Italian goods, because Italy had a large Communist party. This fealty to the working class became two print dresses, a gown, four pairs of shoes, six bras, six lacey lace panties, earrings because they were gold and thus undermined the monetary system of the west, Paris perfumes, and to show that China did not hate the people of America, just its government, a checkered coat that was made on 33rd Street.

The bill came to $875.25. Remo took nine $100 bills from his wallet.

"Cash?" said the sales girl.

"Yes. This is what it looks like. It's green."

She called the floor manager.

"Cash?" said the floor manager.

"Yeah. Money."

Mr. Pelfred, the floor manager, lifted one of the bills to the light, then signalled for another by holding out a hand. He lifted that one to the light also. Then he shrugged.

"What's the matter?" Mei Soong asked Remo.

"I'm paying for something in cash."

"Isn't that what you're supposed to pay in?"

"Well, most purchases are worked through credit cards. You buy whatever you want and they make an impression of your card and send you a bill at the end of the month."

"Oh, yes. Credit cards. The economical exploitation of people through subterfuge, giving them the illusion of purchasing power but making them merely wage slaves to the corporations that issue the cards." Her voice lifted to the ceiling of Lord and Taylor's. "Credit cards should be burned on a fire, along with the people who make them."

"Right on," came from a man in a double breasted suit. A policeman clapped. A woman draped in mink kissed Mei Soong on her cheeks. A businessman raised a clenched fist.

"Well, we'll take your money," said Mr. Pelfred.

"Cash," he yelled out.

"What's that," said one of the clerks.

"It's something they used to use all over. Like what you put in telephones on the street and things."

"Like for buying cigarettes, only more of it, right?"

"Yeah," said the clerk.

Mei Soong wore one of the pink print dresses and the department store packed her greatcoat, her sandals and her gray uniform. She clung to Remo's arm, leaning on him and resting a cheek against his strong shoulders. She watched the clerk fold the coat.

"This is a funny kind of coat. Where's it made?" asked the young girl with fried straw hair and a plastic label that read: "Miss P. Walsh."

"China," said Mei Soong.

"I thought they made nice things in China like silk and stuff."

"The People's Republic of China," said Mei Soong.

"Yeah. Chankee Check. The people's republic of China."

"If you are a servant, then be a servant," said Mei Soong. "Wrap the package and keep your tongue tethered to your mouth."

"You'll want a throne next," Remo whispered to her.

She turned to Remo looking up. "If we are living in a feudal system, then we who are doing secret work should appear to be part of it, correct?"

"I suppose."

Mei Soong smiled a smile of rectification. "Then why should I suffer insolence from a serf?"

"Listen," said Miss P. Walsh. "I don't have to take that crap from you or anyone. You want this package wrapped, then mind your manners. I've never been insulted like this before."

Mei Soong braced herself and in her most imperious manner, said to Miss P. Walsh: "You are a servant and you will serve."

"Listen, Dinko," said Miss P. Walsh. "We got a union around here and we don't have to take that kind of crap from anyone. Now you talk nice or you're getting this coat in your face."

Mr. Pelfred was telling his assistant manager about the cash purchases when he heard the commotion. Up running he came, hippity, hippity, his black shiny shoes pattering along the gray marble floors, his breath puffing from his fatty, shiny face, his hands atwitter.

"Will you please?" he said to Miss P. Walsh.

"Watcher mouth," yelled Miss P. Walsh. "Steward," she screamed. A gaunt hard woman in iron tweed stomped to the cluster around the packing of the greatcoat. "What's going on here?" she said.

"It's not a grievance, please," said Mr. Pelfred.

"I don't have to take this crap from customers or anyone. We got a union," said Miss P. Walsh.

"What's going on?" repeated the gaunt woman.

"There's been a minor disagreement," said Mr. Pelfred.

"I been crapped on by this customer," said Miss P. Walsh, pointing to Mei Soong who stood erect and serene, as if witnessing a squabble between her upstairs and downstairs maids.

"What happened honey?" said the gaunt woman. "Exactly what happened?"

"I was wrapping this funny coat for her and then she told me to tie my tongue or something. She was real aristocratic and she crapped on me. Just plain crapped on me."

131

The gaunt woman stared hatefully at Mr. Pelfred. "We don't have to put up with this, Mr. Pelfred. She does not have to wait on this customer and if you order her to, this whole store is gonna shut down. Tight."

Mr. Pelfred's hands fluttered. "All right. All right. I'll do the wrapping myself."

"You can't," said the gaunt woman. "You're not in the union."

"Fascist pig," said Mei Soong coolly. "The masses have seen their exploitation and are breaking their chains of oppression."

"And you, lotus blossom," said the gaunt woman, "button your lip and get your friggin' coat out the friggin' door or you're going out the friggin' window, along with your sexy looking boyfriend. And if he doesn't like it, he's going out with you."

Remo raised his hands. "I'm a lover, not a fighter."

"You look like it, gigolo," the gaunt woman said.

Mei Soong slowly looked to Remo. "Are you going to allow these insults to be heaped upon me?"

"Yes," said Remo. Her golden face flushed pink and with great chill, she said: "All right. Let's go. Pick up the coat and dresses."

"You take half of them," said Remo.

"You take the coat."

"All right," said Remo. He looked mournfully at Miss P. Walsh. "I wonder if you could do me a big favor. We have a long way to go and if you'd put the coat in a box of some sort, I'd really appreciate it. Anything would do."

"Oh, sure," said Miss P. Walsh. "Hey, look, it might rain. I'll double wrap it. We got a special kind of paper in the back room that's im-pregnant with chemicals. It'll keep it dry."

When the sales girl had left for the special paper wrapping and Pelfred had, as prissily as possible, marched back toward the elevator, and the gaunt woman had swaggered back to the stock room, Mei Soong said to Remo: "You need not have groveled before her."

132

And on their way back to the hotel, she added: "You are a nation without virtue." But she warmed in the lobby and by the time they had returned to their rooms where Chiun sat atop his luggage, she was bubbling over with enthusiasm about her upcoming visit to the karate school she had heard of and what great fun it would be.

Over her shoulder, Remo winked at Chiun, and told him, "Come on, we're going back to Chinatown. To see a karate demonstration."

Then Remo asked the girl, "Do you want to eat now?"

"No," she said quickly. "After the karate school, then I'll eat."

She did not say "we", Remo noticed. Perhaps she expected that he would not be around for dinner.

CHAPTER EIGHTEEN

"Sir, I must advise you that soon you may not place faith in our efforts concerning the matter."

Smith's voice had passed the stage of tension and chill and was now as calm as the Long Island Sound outside his window, a flat, placid sheet of glass, strangely undisturbed by its usual winds and waves.

It was over. Smith had made the decision which his character demanded, that character for which a dead president had chosen him for an assignment he did not want, that character begun in his youth, before memory, and which told Harold W. Smith that there are things you must do, regardless of your personal welfare.

So it was ending now with his own death. Remo would phone. Dr. Smith would order Remo to tell Chiun to return to Folcroft. Chiun would kill Remo and return to his village of Sinanju by the Central Intelligence Agency.

"You've got to stay with this longer," the President said.

"I cannot do that, sir. The three of them have collected a crowd around them. A line of ours was tapped, fortunately by the FBI. But if they knew for sure who we were, think of how they would be compromised. We are going through our prepared program before it will be too late. That is my decision."

"Would it be possible to leave that person still working?" The President's voice was wavering now.

"No."

"Is it possible that something will go wrong with your plans for destruct?"

"Yes."

"How possible?"

"Slight."

"Then if you fail, I still might be able to count on you. Would that be possible?"

"Yes sir, but I doubt it."

"As President of the United States, I order you, Dr. Smith, not to destruct."

"Goodbye, sir, and good luck."

Smith hung up the special phone with the white dot. Oh, to hold his wife again, to say goodbye to his daughters, to play one more round of golf at the Westchester Country Club. He was so close to breaking 90. Why was golf so important now? Funny. But then why should golf be important in the first place?

Maybe it was good to leave now. No man knew the hour of his death, the Bible said. But Smith would know the exact second. He looked at his watch again. One minute to go. He took the container with the pill from his gray vest pocket. It would do the job.

The pill was white and oblong with beveled edges like a coffin. That was to let people know it was poison and not to be consumed. Smith had learned that when he was six. It was the sort of information that remained with a person. He had not, in his lifetime, ever had use for it.

With his mind now floating in the nether world of faces and words and feelings he had thought he had forgotten, Smith spun the coffin-like pill on the memo that would take the aluminum box to Parsippany, New Jersey.

The central phone rang. Smith picked it up and noticed his hand was trembling and the phone slippery from the perspiration.

"I've got good news for you," came Remo's voice.

"Yes?" said Smith.

"I think I can latch on to our man. And I'm going to where he is."

"Very good," said Dr. Smith. "Nice going. By the way, you can tell Chiun to return to Folcroft."

"Nah," said Remo. "He's gonna work out fine. I know just how to use him."

"Well," said Smith. "He doesn't really fit into the picture now. You send him back."

"No way," said Remo. "I need him now. Don't worry. Everything is going to work out fine."

"Well, then," Smith's voice was calm in appearance, "just tell him that I asked for him to return, okay?"

"No good. I know what you're doing. I tell him that and he'll return, no matter what else I tell him. He's a pro like that."

"You be a pro like that. I want him back now."

"You'll get him tomorrow."

"Tell him today."

"No deal, sweetheart."

"Remo, this is an order. This is an important order."

There was silence at the other end of the phone, an open line to somewhere. Dr. Smith could not afford to give away what he had just given away and yet he had had to try strength.

It didn't work. "Hell, you're always worrying about something. I'll check with you tomorrow. Another day won't cripple you."

"Are you refusing an order?"

"Sue me," came the voice and Smith heard the click of a dead line.

Dr. Smith returned the receiver to the cradle, returned the pill to the little bottle, returned the bottle to his vest, and buzzed his secretary.

"Phone my wife. Tell her I'll be home late for dinner, then phone the club and get me a tee time."

"Yes, sir. About the memo on the shipment of the goods downstairs? Should I send it?"

"Not today," said Dr. Smith.

There was nothing he would be needed for until tomorrow at noon. The only function he had left was to die and take an organization with him. He could not do that until the first step—the death of Remo—was settled. And since he had no other decisions to make, he would go golfing. Of course, under all this pressure, he wouldn't break 80. If he could break 90, that would be an accomplishment under the circumstances of today. Breaking 90 today would be the equivalent of breaking 80 under other circumstances. Because of the seriousness of the day, Smith would allow himself a mulligan. No, two mulligans.

It was a peculiarity of Dr. Harold W. Smith that his honesty and integrity, steel bound unto death, would, when he put a white ball on a wooden tee, dissolve into marshmallow.

By the time he waggled himself into a solid stance at the first tee, Dr. Smith had given himself four strokes for his impending demise, winter rules because of his lower body temperature, and any putt within six feet of the pin. The last advantage still awaited a rationale, but Dr. Smith was sure he would have it by the first green.

CHAPTER NINETEEN

Bernoy Jackson packed a .357 Magnum revolver into his attache case, a pistol known as a cannon with a handle. He would have taken a real cannon, but it would not have fit, either into his attache case, or into the main floor of Bong Rhee's Karate Dojo.

He would have liked to have brought with him five button men from his own organization and perhaps, an enforcer or two from organizations in Brooklyn and the Bronx.

What he really wanted, and he knew this very well when he pulled his customized Fleetwood from the garage around the corner and clipped a hydrant on his way out, was to not be going to the school at all.

As the $14,000 gray vehicle with sun roof, stereo, bar, phone and color TV, moved down 125th Street toward the East River Drive, he thought for a moment that if he turned north on the drive he could keep going. Of course, he would have to go back to his pad first, and remove cash from the hidden safe behind the third plant. What was that? $120,000. It was just a fraction of his worth, but he would be alive to spend it. Then he could start again, take his time, set up slowly. He had the bankroll for a good numbers operation and he knew how to run it.

The wheel was sweat-slippery in his hands as he passed under the Penn Central Railroad tracks. He was nine when he realized those tracks did not lead to all the faraway wonderful places in the world but just to upstate New York with Ossining on its way and an awful lot of towns that didn't want Nigger boys like Bernoy Jackson.

His grandmother had been so wise: "The man ain't ever gonna do you right, boy."

And he believed it. And when he should have believed it most, eight years before, he didn't. And now, as befitting life in Harlem, having made the wrong decision, he was going to die for it.

Jackson turned the air conditioner to high, but found little comfort. He was simultaneously chilled and perspiring. He wiped his right hand against the soft dry material of the seat. His first Cadillac was lined with white fur, an incredibly silly venture, but one he had dreamed of. The fur wore too quickly and the car was vandalized five times in the first month, even in the garage.

Now his Fleetwood was gray with all the good things neatly hidden. He would be at the East River Drive soon. And when he turned right to go south, to go downtown, to go to his death, there would be no turning back. That was the big difference between Harlem and white America.

In white America, people could make a major mistake and recoup. In Harlem, your first big one was your last big one. It had seemed so easy eight years before when he should have remembered his grandmother's advice and taken counsel of his own beliefs. But the money was so good.

He was sipping a Big Apple special, three shots of scotch for the price of two, when another runner, they were all small time then, laid the word on him that a man wanted to see him.

He had purposely continued to sip his scotch slowly, showing no great concern. When he was finished, with great effort at being casual he left the Big Apple bar, out onto chilly Lenox Avenue, where a black man in a gray suit sat in a gray car and nodded to him.

"Sweet Shiv?" said the man, opening the door.

"Yeah," said Jackson, not moving closer, but keeping his hand in the right pocket of his jacket over the neat .25 caliber Beretta.

"I want to give you two numbers and $100," the man

said. "The first number you play tomorrow. The second number you phone tomorrow night. Play only $10 and don't play with your boss, Derellio."

He should have asked why he was the lucky recipient. He should have been more suspicious at the man knowing his nature so well, knowing that having been told to play a number with all the money, he would have played none of it. Having been just given a number he would have ignored it. But having been given $100 to play $10, he would risk the $10, just to make the phone call more interesting.

Jackson's first thought was that he was being set up to break a banker. But not on $10. Did the man in the car really want him to play the $100 and another $500 on top of that?

If so, why pick Sweet Shiv? Sweet Shiv wasn't going to put his own money into something he couldn't control. That was for little old ladies with their quarters and their dreams. That was what the numbers were in Harlem. The dream. If people really wanted to make money they would go to the Man's numbers, the stock market, where the odds were in your favor. But the Man's numbers were too real, it reminded you you didn't have nothing worth betting and you'd never make it out of the mud.

The numbers, however, they were pure sweet fantasy. You bought a day of dreaming of what you'd do with $5,400 for $10. And for a quarter, you got $135 worth of groceries, or rent, or a new suit, or a good taste if that was your pleasure. Or whatever your pleasure.

Nothing would ever replace the numbers in Harlem. Nothing would ever stop them, not unless someone came along with a new instant dream, payable the next day at the corner candy store.

Jackson bet the number and won. Then he phoned the other number.

"Now," came the voice, "bet 851 and 857, small. Play it with your boss, Derellio, and tell your players to play those numbers too. And phone back tomorrow night."

Eight fifty one paid off but the hit was not that big because Jackson's players did not trust him. Not that they thought he was untrustful, Jackson knew, but that they did not really have a handle on him.

When he phoned the number again, the voice said: "The number tomorrow is 962. Tell your people you have the strongest hunch ever. And tell them you can only take so much, they'll have to go to Derellio personally. And play the number straight."

The play the next day was heavy. Big. And when 962 appeared in the day's parimutuel handle on the next to the last page of the Daily News, Derellio was broken. He had been hit for $480,000 and had not laid off any of the bets.

The next night, the voice said: "Meet me on the ferry going towards Staten Island that leaves in an hour."

It was bitter cold on the ferry, but the man who had been in the car, seemed not to mind the cold. He was well trussed in fur lined coat and boots and furlined field cap. He gave Jackson an attache case.

"There's half a million in there. Pay off all Derellio's winners. And phone me again tomorrow night."

"What's your game?" asked Jackson.

"Would you believe," the man said, "that the more I learn of what I do, the less I know why I'm doing it."

"You don't talk like a brother."

"Ah, that's the problem of the black bourgeoisie, my friend. Goodbye."

"Wait a minute," said Jackson, hopping up and down on the deck of the ferry, beating his arms for warmth while trying to balance the attache case between his legs, "what if I take a walk with this bread, man?"

"Well," said the man wearily, "I sort of figure you're pretty smart. And you're not going to walk until you know who you're walking from. And the more you know, the less you're going to want to walk."

"You don't make sense, dude."

"I haven't made sense since I took this job. Just accuracy." The black man said goodbye again and walked away. So Jackson had paid off the players and taken over the bank. If they could give him a half million to throw away, they could give him a million for himself. Besides, then he would walk.

But he did not walk. He did not walk when he received his bankroll. He did not walk, even when he was told to stand on a street corner one night, only to be told by a white man an hour later, "You can go now." Derellio and two of his henchmen were discovered with their necks broken in a nearby store a half hour later, and Sweet Shiv Jackson suddenly had a reputation for having killed three men with his bare hands which vastly increased the honesty of his numbers runners. And all it cost was just a little favor every now and then for the weary-voiced black dude.

Just little favors. Usually information, and sometimes it was putting this device here or that there, or providing an absolutely unshakeable witness for a trial or making sure another witness had money to leave town. And within a year, his main job was running an information network that stretched from the Polo Grounds to Central Park.

Even his vacation in the Bahamas was not his own. He found himself in a classroom with an old white man with a Hungarian accent discussing in terms he had not used, things Jackson thought only the street knew. There were names for things like seals, links, cells, variables of accuracy. He had liked variables of accuracy. In street terms, it was "where he coming from?" It was cool.

And then his network one fine autumn day was suddenly very interested in Orientals. Nothing specific. Just anything about Orientals that might come up.

And then the dude reappeared and informed Sweet Shiv that now he would pay back in full for his good fortune. He would kill a man whose picture was in this envelope and he would kill him at the Bong Rhee karate dojo. The man had insisted that Sweet Shiv not open the envelope until he left.

And so for the second time, Sweet Shiv saw the face, the high cheekbones, the deep brown eyes, the thin lips. The first time had been when he stood on a corner he had been told to stand on at a certain time, and the man had come out of the shop where Derellios' body was found later and had said simply: "You can go now."

He was now going to see that face again, and this time Sweet Shiv was supposed to put a bullet in it. And Sweet Shiv knew as he turned south into Manhattan on the East River Drive that he was going to be wasted.

Somewhere a machine he had been part of was coming apart. And that machine belonged to the man. And the man had decided that one of its little black wheels was now going to be a piston. And if you lose a little black wheel trying to be a piston, well, what the hell, what's one Nigger more or less?

Sweet Shiv turned right on 14th Street, then made a U turn in the middle of the block, got back on the East Side Highway and headed north.

He had $800 in his pocket. He would not stop at his home to pick up his cash, he would not even bother to seal his car when he reached Rochester. He would leave nothing by which anyone could trace him.

Let them have the money. Let some stranger take the car. Let them have everything. He was going to live.

"Baby," he said to himself, "they really had you going."

He felt somewhat happy that he was going to live another day. He felt this way until just before the Major Deegan Highway leading to the New York Thruway and upstate. A black family was sitting by their stalled 1957 Chevrolet, a paintworn, chipped, banged-up leftover of a car which had apparently surrendered its ghost for the last time. But Jackson figured he could make it run again.

He pulled it over, the wide soft wheels with their magnificent springs and shocks, taking the curb like a twig. He stopped on the grass which rose to a fence which separated the Bronx from the Major Deegan a few miles south of Yankee Stadium, the Black and Puerto Rican Bronx with dying buildings teeming with life.

He opened the door and got out into the stale smelling air and looked at the family. Four youngsters had been playing with a can, four youngsters in clothes so casual they looked as if they had been rejected by the Salvation Army. These four youngsters, one of whom might have been Sweet Shiv Jackson 15 years before, stopped playing to look at him.

The father sat by the front left fender, his back to the flat bald tire, his face cemented in resignation. A woman, old as flesh and weary as millstones, snored in the front seat.

"How you doin', brother?"

"Fine," said the man looking up. "You got a tire that will fit?"

"I got a whole car that will fit."

"Who I got to kill?"

"Nobody."

"Sounds fine, but. . . ."

"But what?"

"But I wouldn't make it to your wheels, man. You got company."

Sweet Shiv, maintaining his cool, slowly scanned behind him. A simple black sedan had pulled up behind his Fleetwood. From the near window, a black face stared at him. It was the dude, the man on the ferry, the man who had given him the numbers and the methods, and the orders.

Jackson's stomach dissolved into strings. His arms hung leaden as though enervated by electricity.

The man stared directly into his eyes and shook his head. All Bernoy (Sweet Shiv) Jackson could do was nod. "Yowsah," he said, and the man in the car smiled.

Jackson turned to the man on the grass and carefully peeled from a roll of bills in his pocket all but $20.

The man eyed him suspiciously.

"Take it," said Jackson.

The man did not move.

"You got more smarts than I got, brother. Take it. I won't need it. I'm a dead man."

Still no movement.

So Sweet Shiv Jackson dropped the money in the front seat of the remnant of a 1957 Chevrolet and returned to his Fleetwood which still had one payment on it outstanding. The life of Bernoy (Sweet Shiv) Jackson.

CHAPTER TWENTY

Remo Williams spotted the man with the .357 Magnum first. Then the man with the very big bulge in his Oscar de la Renta suit spotted Remo. Then the man smiled weakly.

Remo smiled too.

The man stood before the Bong Rhee karate school, a walkup entrance with a painted sign telling people to walk up one flight and that when they traversed the stairs they would be in one of the leading schools of self defense in the Western Hemisphere.

Remo said, "What's your name?"

"Bernoy Jackson."

"How do you want to die, Bernoy?"

"No way, man," said Bernoy honestly.

"Then tell me who sent you."

Bernoy recounted the story. His black boss. The numbers that hit. Then standing on the corner near where three men were killed. And the information.

"That corner. That's where I saw you."

"That's right," Remo said. "I probably should kill you now."

Sweet Shiv went for the gun. Remo snapped out his knuckles into the man's wrist. Jackson grimaced in pain and clutched his wrist. His pain brought sweat to his large forehead. "All I gotta say, honkie, is you a bunch of mean bastards. You the meanest, toughest bastards on this planet earf."

"I hope so," Remo said. "Now beat it."

Sweet Shiv turned and walked away and Remo watched him go, quietly sympathizing with the man who was obviously a CURE agent and did not know it. Remo had been framed. Bernoy Jackson had been bought. But they were brothers under the skin somehow, and so Jackson lived.

What hurt was that Remo had been marked for death. And now he could trust no one. But why had they sent that Jackson? CURE must be compromised beyond saving. Then why go through with the search for Liu? What else was there to do?

Remo went into the door of the karate school. He felt Chiun follow him up the creaky wood steps in the narrow stairway, boxed in by grease-coated, dust-catching green paint. A lightbulb at the top of the stairs illuminated a red painted arrow. The paint was fresh. Mei Soong followed Chiun.

"Oh how wonderful it is to work with you, Remo," Chiun said.

"Drop dead."

"Not only are you a detective and secretary of state but now you are becoming socially aware. Why did you let that man walk away?"

"Swallow your spit."

"He recognized you. And you let him go."

"Suck cyanide."

Remo paused at the top of the stairs, Chiun and Mei Soong waiting behind him.

"Are you contemplating the stairwell or a new cause of social justice?" Chiun's face was serene.

It would be Chiun. Remo had always known it, but did not want to believe it. Who else could do it? Not that Jackson. Yet Chiun had not terminated him.

That Chiun had not been able to was out of the question. The thought momentarily arose in Remo's mind that Chiun might have refrained because of affection for Remo. The thought was as fleeting as it was absurd. If Remo had to go, Chiun would do it. Just another job.

Then it was the message that had failed. It had not reached Chiun. Remo thought of the phone call to Smith, and his insistence that Remo tell Chiun to return to Folcroft. Of course that was the signal—and Remo had not transmitted it.

The course for Remo now was clear. Just throw a shot to the frail yellow throat in the hallway, now while they were pressed together. Stun him. Kill him. And then run. And keep running.

That was his only hope.

Chiun looked up at him quizzically.

"Well," he said, "are we to reside here forever to become an element of the scenery?"

"No," said Remo with heaviness in his voice. "We're going inside."

"You will find it a most attractive and rewarding experience to witness the martial arts," Mei Soong said.

Chiun smiled. Mei Soong pushed past them and opened the door. Chiun and Remo followed, into the large low-ceilinged white room with sunlight coming in over the backs of large pictures in the front windows of what had once been a loft. Off to the right were the usual paraphernalia of karate schools, sandbags, and roofing tiles, and a large box filled with beans, used for toughening the fingertips.

Mei Soong confidently walked over to a small glass-windowed office with a bare desk upon which sat a young Oriental man in white floppy karate suit tied with a red belt. His head was shaven almost clean, his features smooth, his expression calm with the kind of calmness that comes with years of training and years of discipline.

Chiun whispered to Remo: "He is very good. One of only eight true red belts. A very young man in his early 40's."

"He looks 20."

"He is very, very good. And would give you an interesting exercise, if you chose to allow it to be interesting. His father, however, would give you more than an interesting exercise."

"Danger?"

"You are an insulting young man. How dare you think

148

that someone I trained these many years would be in danger of such a red belt? What insulting stupidity. I have given you years of my life and you dare to say that." Chiun's voice lowered slightly. "You are a very stupid man and also forgetful. You fail to remember that anyone taught pure attack can defeat karate, even a man in a wheelchair. Karate is an art. A minimal art. Its weakness is that it is a killing art only at time, a small slice of the circle. We approach the circle. They do not."

Remo watched Mei Soong, her back to him. The Oriental in the red belt listened closely. Then he looked up, seeing Remo but concentrating on Chiun. He left his office, still peering at Chiun and when he was five feet away, his mouth opened and blood appeared to drain from his face.

"No," he said. "No."

"I see, Mr. Kyoto, that you have earned young yōur red belt. Your father must be very proud. Your family has always loved dancing. I am honored to be in your presence and extend utmost cordialities to your honorable father." Chiun bowed slightly.

Kyoto did not move. Then, recollecting his functions, he bowed extremely deeply in a smooth graceful motion, then backed away quickly until he bumped into Mei Soong.

From the wall farthest from the window, where a sign read dressing room, a file of men emerged through a door, seven black men in phalanx, all wearing black belts. They moved with grace and silence, their white karate uniforms blurring against each other, creating a mass which made definition more difficult.

"Go back, go back," yelled Kyotō. But they kept coming until they had surrounded Chiun and Remo.

"It is all right, Mr. Kyoto," said Chiun. "I am just an innocent observer. I give you my word I will not get involved."

Kyoto glanced back at him. Chiun nodded politely, smiling.

One of the black men spoke. He was tall, six-feet four, 245 pounds and no flab. His face looked carved of ebony. He was grinning.

"We of the third world has nothin' against a brother of the third world. We wants the honkey."

Remo glanced at Mei Soong. Her face was frozen, her lips clamped thin. She was undoubtedly going through more emotional tension than Remo who was just going to do what he was trained to do. A woman in love betraying her lover was an airport of signals.

"Learned master of all arts, am I to understand you will not intrude yourself?" asked Kyoto.

"I will stand aside to witness the spectacle of all these people attacking one poor white man. For I can see that is what they are prepared to do," Chiun said this almost as a sermon, then pointing a shaking forefinger at Mei Soong, he added: "And you, faithless woman, luring this unsuspecting young man into this den of death. For shame."

"Hey, old man. Don't feel sorry for no honkey. He our enemy," said the man of the ebony face.

Remo, listened to the interchange, yawned. Chiun's dramatics did not impress him. He had seen Chiun play humbled before. Now Chiun was setting them up for him, although from their swaggering they appeared not to need setting up.

"Move over," said the leader to Chiun, "or we'll move on over you."

"I beg a boon," implored Chiun. "I know this poor man who is about to die. I wish to say goodbye to him."

"Don't let him, he'll pass him a gun or something," yelled one of the blacks.

"I have no weapon. I am a man of peace and solitude, a frail flower cast upon the harsh rocky soil of conflict."

"Hey, what he talk?" came the voice of the man with the largest Afro, a spray of coiled black weeds exploding in all directions from his tan head.

"He say he ain't carrying," said the leader.

150

"He look funny for a gook."

"Don't say gook. He third world," said the leader. "Yes, old man. Say goodbye to the honkey. The revolution is here."

Remo watched the crowd raise their fists to the ceiling of fluorescent lights and wondered how much he would reduce New York City's welfare bill. Unless, of course, they were somewhat competent in which case he would reduce the crime rate.

The group was now giving each other fancy handshakes, saying "Pass the power, brother."

Remo looked at Chiun and shrugged. Chiun beckoned Remo's head to lower. "You do not know how important this is. It is very important. I know personally Kyoto's father. You have some bad habits which inhibit grace when you become excited. I have not corrected them because they will work themselves out and to change them now would inhibit your attack. But what you must avoid at all costs is a full energy attack, because these habits will surely show, and Kyoto's father will hear about your lack of grace. A companion of mine lacking grace."

"Gosh, you have problems," Remo said.

"Do not joke. This is important to me. Perhaps you do not have pride in yourself, but I have pride in myself. I do not wish to be embarrassed. It is not like white or black men were watching but a yellow man of red belt whose father knows me personally."

"And it's not like I'm going against Amos and Andy," Remo whispered. "These guys look tough."

Chiun peered briefly around Remo's shoulder at the group, some of whom were taking off their shirts to show their muscles, for Mei Soong's benefit.

"Amos and Andy," Chiun said, "whoever they are. Now please, I ask this favor of you now."

"Will you give me a favor in return?"

"All right. All right. But remember. The most important thing is not to embarrass my instructional methods."

Chiun bowed and even pretended to brush away a tear.

He stepped back, signalling Mei Soong and Kyoto to join him. One of the men who had removed his shirt showed fine round muscled shoulders and a good rippling stomach stacked with rows of muscles like a washboard. A weight lifter, thought Remo. Nothing.

The man swaggered to Chiun, Kyoto and Mei Soong, signalling they should go no further.

"He is my pupil of a few days," Chiun confided openly to Kyoto, while pointing to Remo.

"You stay where you is. All of you," said the well muscled man. "Ah don't wants to hurt no brother of the third world."

Remo heard Kyoto snort laughter.

"I take it," Chiun said, "that these are the students of your honorable house."

"They have walked in," came Kyoto's voice.

"Walk in?" Remo heard the guard behind him say. "We been working out here for years."

"Thank you," said Chiun. "Now we will see what years of Kyoto instruction does in comparison with just a few humble words from the house of Sinanju. Begin if you will."

Remo heard Kyoto groan. "Why must my ancestors be forced to witness this?"

"Don't worry," came the black guard's voice. "We'll do you up proud. Real proud. Black power proud."

"My heart trembles before your black power," said Chiun, "and my respect for the House of Kyoto knows no bounds. Woe is me and my friend."

The seven black men moved wide for the kill. Remo set for the attack, his weight centered for instant movement in any direction.

It was funny. Here Chiun was warning him about performance, and Remo needed no warning. It was the first time Chiun would see his pupil in action and Remo wanted, as he wanted few things, to win praise from the little father.

One should not concern oneself with appearances but results. That is how Remo's training differed from karate, but now he was worried about appearances. And that could be deadly.

CHAPTER TWENTY ONE

There were seven and Remo prepared to work right, slant in left, pick up two, then come back across, pick up one, and work it from there. It wasn't necessary.

The biggest one, with the ebony face, stepped into the circle. His Afro was manicured like a well-tended hedge, and he stood with his forearms held forward, wrists limp. One of the blacks behind him, who did not practice the Preying Mantis attack of the school of Kung Fu, laughed.

Large, strong men rarely used the Praying Mantis. It was an attack small men used to compensate. If the big man with the flaming Afro should slip past Remo's attack, Remo would be dead with one blow.

"Hey, Piggy," said the black who had laughed. "You look faggy."

Piggy moved fast for a big man, extending one leg, then moving a stroke towards Remo's head. Remo was under the stroke, driving fingers into the solar plexus, then back up to catch the sirloin roll neck with a down stroke, knee up to smash the face and set it up for a follow through with the fingers extended into the temple. The body hit the mat almost silently, the face still surprised. The left hand remained curved.

Then there were six, six stunned black faces, eyes widening. Then someone had the correct idea to attack en masse. It looked like a race riot in martial arts robes. "Get the honkey bastard. Kill Whitey. Get whitey."

Their screams echoed in the hall. Remo glanced to Chiun to see if there was approval. Mistake. A black hand came into his face and he saw darkness and stars, but as he felt himself going down, he saw the white of the mat,

154

and saw the arms and legs and black hands with lighter palms, and felt a foot come up toward his groin.

He brought one hand up behind the kneecap, and using his fall flipped the body attached to the knee over his head. He brought a foot up into a groin and rolled. As he did so, he moved to his feet, caught an Afro and cracked down into it, smashing a skull.

A voiceless body hit the mat. A black belt launched an attack with a foot shot. Remo grabbed the ankle and kept it going behind his head and brought his thumb up sharply into the man's back, damaging a kidney and flinging him to the side, shrieking in pain. Now there were four, and they weren't as anxious to get whitey. One was downright brotherly as he nursed his broken knee. Three black belts surrounded Remo in a semi-circle.

"All at once. Attack. On three," said one, making sense. He was very dark, black as night and his beard was scraggly. His eyes had no whites, just black fires of hate. Perspiration beaded his forehead. By showing his hate so openly, he had blown his cool.

"Ain't like the movie, Shaft, is it, Sambo?" said Remo. And he laughed.

"Mother," said the black belt to Remo's left.

"Is that a plea? Or half a word?" Remo asked.

"One," called out the man with hate.

"Two," called out the man with hate.

"Three," called out the man with hate, and he went with a foot, the other two with straight ahead punches.

Remo was down beneath them, slipping behind the man who hated. He spun around, snatched his foot and kept spinning him to the bean box where students and instructors toughened their fingertips by ramming them into eight inches of beans. Remo rammed his hand into the box very quickly, but it did not reach the bottom.

It did not reach the bottom of the box because under his hand was the hate-filled face. It no longer hated because jammed into the box at that speed, it was no longer a face. It was a pulp. Beans had been driven into the eyes.

From above, it looked as if the black belt who had weakened to hate under the pressure of fear was drinking from the box deeply, the beans covering his head. Blood seeped up through the beans, swelling them.

Remo did a waltz skip to a pile of tiles with the other two black belts swinging about his head and toward his back. He scooped up two curved gray tiles from the pile and began to whistle, and as he dodged blows and kicks, he began clacking the curved bricks in rhythm to the melody.

He spun around one blow and brought the two bricks, one in each hand, together, with an Afro between them. Directly in the middle of the Afro was a head. The two bricks made valiant effort to meet. But they cracked. So did the head in the Afro between them.

The Afro with the open-mouthed head went to the mat. The remnants of the tiles went into the air. The last black standing threw an elbow that missed and then said, eloquently:

"Sheeit."

He stood there, his arms hanging, his forehead perspiring. "Ah don't know what you got, man, but Ah can't take it."

"Yeah," said Remo. "Sorry."

"Up yours, honkey," said the man, breathing heavily.

"That's the business, sweetheart," said Remo and as the man made one last desperate lunge, Remo shattered his throat with a back slash.

He untied the black belts as the corpse staggered by and walked over to the man with the broken knee who was trying to crawl to the door. He dangled the belt in front of his face.

"Want to win another one fast?"

"No man, I don't want nuthin'."

"Don't you want to wipe out whitey?"

"No, man," cried the crawling black belt.

"Ah, c'mon. Don't tell me you're one of those who save his militancy for deserted subways and classrooms?"

156

"Man, Ah don't want no trouble. Ah ain't done nuthin'. You brutalizing."

"You mean when you mug someone, that's revolution. But when you get mugged, that's brutality."

"No, man." The black covered his head awaiting some sort of blow. Remo shrugged.

"Give him the black belt of the dojo of Kyoto," sang out Chiun. Remo saw anger flood the face of Kyoto, but it was quickly controlled.

"Unless, of course," Chiun said sweetly to Kyoto, "you of years of experience would care to teach the martial arts to my humble student of just a few moments?"

"That is not a humble student," said Kyoto. "And you did not teach him art, but the methods of Sinanju."

"All the house of Sinanju had to work with was a white man. But in our small way, we attempt to do the best we can with whatever is given us." The black belt with the broken knee was now scurrying into a dressing room out a side door, which slammed shut behind him. Kyoto's eyes followed the sound and Chiun said, "That man has the instincts of a champion. I will tell your honorable father how successful you are in teaching track and field. He will be happy that you have deserted dangerous sports."

Remo folded the black belt in his hands carefully, walked over and flipped it to Kyoto. "Maybe you can sell it to somebody else."

The dojo looked as if it had just surfaced from a whirlpool that had struck in the middle of a class. Chiun looked happy, but he said: "Pitiful. Your left hand still fails to extend properly."

Mei Soong was ashen-faced.

"I thought . . . I thought . . . Americans were soft."

"They are," snickered Chiun.

"Thanks for bringing me here," Remo said. "Any other places you wish to visit?"

Mei Soong paused. "Yes," she finally said. "I'm hungry."

CHAPTER TWENTY-TWO

In the long march, there had been nothing like it. In the days of hiding in the caves of Yenan there had been nothing like it. And there was no answer in the thoughts of Mao tse Tung. Even in the spirit of Mao, there was no answer.

General Liu forced himself to accept with politeness the news from the messenger. In the decadent monarchist regimes of the past, the evil of the news would have fallen on the head of its bearer. But this was a new age, and General Liu simply said: "You may go and thank you, comrade."

There had been nothing like it before. He watched the messenger salute and depart, shutting the door behind him, leaving General Liu in the windowless room which smelled of oil on metal and had but one chair and a bed, and very poor ventilation.

Other generals might live in splendor, but a people's general could never aggrandize himself. Other generals might live in palace houses like warlords, but not him. Not a real people's general who had buried his brothers in mountains and left a sister in a winter's snow, who had at 13 been requisitioned for service in the Mandarin's fields, just as his sister had been requisitioned for service in the Mandarin's bed.

General Liu was a great general of the people, not in his pride but in his experience. He could smell the quality of a division 10 miles away. He had seen armies rape and pillage, and he had seen armies build towns and schoolhouses. He had seen a lone man annihilate a platoon. But he had never seen what he was seeing now. And in comfort-loving America, of all places.

He looked down again at the note in his hands, and as he had looked at other notes during the three days he had been in hiding.

First, there were the hired gangsters in Puerto Rico. Not revolutionaries, but competent. And they had failed.

Then there was Ricardo de Estrana y Montaldo y Ruiz Guerner, of personal experience a man who had never failed. And he had failed.

And there was the Wah Ching street gang. And it had failed.

And when guns and gangs had failed, there were the great hands of the karate black belt.

He looked down at the note in his hands. And now that too had failed. They had all failed in both their missions: to eliminate those who were trying to find the general and to bring to him his bride of only one year.

And if General Liu and his men continued to fail, his people would cast themselves at the feet of the peacemakers in Peking, ready to forget the years of hardship and to end the revolution before it was complete.

Did they not know that Mao was just a man? A great man, but just a man and men grow old and weary and wish to die in peace?

Did they not see that this step backwards, making peace with imperialism, was a retreat, just when the battle was being won? With victory in their mouths, would they now succumb to the son of a mandarin, the premier, and sit at the same table with the dying beast of capitalism?

Not if General Liu could stop it. General Liu would not have peace. The premier had misjudged his cunning, misjudged even his motives.

He had been careful not to let himself be seen in China as a leader of the war faction. He was just a people's general, until chosen by the premier to arrange safe journey for his trip to see the swine American President. He had quietly arranged for the deaths on the transport

159

plane, and when that did not halt plans for the premier's visit, he volunteered to go to America himself. And then after changing to western garb, he had shot his own guards and slipped alone, unnoticed onto the train which had brought him here.

It should have been easy to stay hidden during the seven days of grace the premier had given the Americans. But this impossible American could not be denied, and even now was probably closing in on General Liu. When his followers heard of the escape from the karate dojo, they would lose heart. They must be firmed up.

General Liu sat down on his hard cot. He would go through his plans three times, thinking over the details from three angles. Then he would speak to his people.

And then, when he was ready, he would act with thoroughness, and when the plan proved successful, he would hold in his arms once more, Mei Soong, the beautiful flower, the only pleasure of his life outside duty.

This plan must not fail. Not even before this impossible American who had once again revived the ancient fairy tales of an ancient China. Yes. He must first discredit the fairy tales.

General Liu rose from his cot and banged on the heavy steel door. A man in drab army type clothing opened it. "I will meet with the leaders immediately," General Liu said. Then he shut the door with a clang and heard the lock fall into place.

Within minutes, all had gathered, standing in the little airless room. The early arrivals were fidgeting for want of fresh air. Some perspired and General Liu noticed how fat some faces were, how flaccid, how pale. They were not like the people of the long march. They were like the people of Chiang Kai Shek and his soft running dogs.

Well, General Liu had often led unfit men into combat. He talked now to them . . . of the long struggle and of the dark hours and how these had been overcome. He talked of hunger and cold and how these had been overcome. He spoke to the pride in the hearts of the people before him

160

and when they no longer suffered from the heat or the air but were overcome by revolutionary fervor, he hit his target where he wished to hit his target.

"Comrades," he said in the outlawed Cantonese dialect, looking around the room and meeting their eyes, "we who have accomplished so much, how can we now fall prey to a child's fairy tale? Was not the winter in the caves of Yenan fiercer than a fairy tale? Were not the armies of Chiang and his running dogs fiercer than a fairy tale? Are not the armaments of modern times fiercer than a fairy tale?"

"Yes, yes," came the voices. "True. How true."

"Then why," asked General Liu, "should we fear the fairy tales of Sinanju?"

One young man said triumphantly: "Never fear suffering. Never fear death. Never fear, least of all, fairy tales."

But an old man, in what were once the clothes of the mainland, said: "He kills like the night tigers of Sinanju. This he does."

"I fear this man," General Liu said, stunning his audience. "But I fear him as a man, not as a fairy tale. He is a formidable man, but we have defeated formidable men before. But he is no night tiger from Sinanju, because there is no such thing. It is just a village in the People's Republic of Korea. You, comrade Chen. You have been there. Tell us of Sinanju."

A middle aged man in a dark, single breasted business suit, with a face of steel and a haircut that looked an accident of shrub shears, came forward to stand by General Liu. He faced the men crowded into the stuffy room.

"I have been to Sinanju. I have spoken to the people of Sinanju. They were poor and exploited before the glorious revolution. Now they are beginning to enjoy the fruits of freedom and. . . ."

"The legend," interrupted General Liu. "Tell them of the legend."

"Yes," said the man. "I sought out the Master of Sinanju. What master, the people asked me. The master of the night tigers, I said to them. There is no such thing, they said. If there were, would we be so poor? And I left. And even the Spaniard who once worked for us said he could not find the Master of Sinanju. So why should we believe there is such a one?"

"Did you put money in the pockets of the people of Sinanju?" asked the old man who had spoken before.

"I did not," the man responded angrily. "I represented the revolution, not the New York Stock Exchange."

"The people of Sinanju are money worshippers," the old man said. "If you had offered money and they had still said no, I would be more heartened."

General Liu spoke up. "The American we are talking about is a man whose face is pale as dough. Would the master of Sinanju make of a pale face a night tiger? Even in the legend, only people of the village of Sinanju become night tigers."

"You are wrong, Comrade general. The legend says that there will someday be a master so enamored of money that for great wealth he will teach a pale face who has died all the secrets of Sinanju. He will make of him a night tiger, but the most awesome of night tigers. He will make him kin to the gods of India, kin to Shiva, the destroyer."

There was silence in the room. And no one moved.

"And within an hour," said General Liu, "this Destroyer, this dead man, will be lying on this cot. And I will give you the privilege of executing his legendary body. Unless, of course, our revolution must be cancelled because of a fairy tale."

This broke the tension, and everyone laughed. Everyone but the old man.

He said, "The white man has been seen with an elderly Korean."

"His interpreter."

"He could be the Master of Sinanju."

"Nonsense," General Liu said. "He is a frail flower

162

ready for interment." To save the old man the great hurt of losing face, General Liu bowed to him in the old way. "Come, comrade. You have done too much for the revolution, not to join with us now in our moment of glory." He signalled for the man to stay. The others chattered with confidence as they filed through the narrow steel door. They were a unit again.

General Liu went to the door and closed it and motioned the old man to sit on his cot. He placed himself on the single chair in the room and said: "This Sinanju. I have heard the legend too, but I do not believe it."

The old man nodded. His eyes were old as shale, his face as stiffening leather.

"But I have been confronted by other things I find hard to believe," Liu continued. "Supposing this fairy tale, this Shiva the Destroyer, exists. Does the legend tell of a weakness?"

"Yes," said the old man. "He is influenced by the moon of justice."

Liu lashed his anger to the controlling rod, withholding the storm inside him. How often he had been forced to deal gently with the archaic poetry of thought that chained his people to poverty and superstition. He forced himself to speak gently.

"Are there any other weaknesses?"

"Yes."

"How can he be overcome?"

The old man said quickly and simply, "Poison." But he added cautiously: "One must not trust poison. His body is strange and may recover from the poison in time. Poison to weaken him, and then a knife or gun."

"Poison, you say?"

"Yes."

"Then, poison it shall be."

"You have a way to deliver this poison to his system?"

They were interrupted by a knock at the door. A messenger entered and handed Liu a note.

He read it and beamed expansively at the old man: "Yes, comrade. A lovely, charming delicate way to deliver this poison. She has just arrived upstairs."

CHAPTER TWENTY-THREE

It was the best beef in oyster sauce Remo had ever tasted. A special dark flavor that raised the senses to the thin strips of beef bathing in brown syrup. Remo speared another dark sliver with the stainless steel fork and twirled it in the oyster sauce, then lifted it, dripping, to his mouth, where he let it rest, tingling, vibrant and delicious.

"I have never enjoyed any dish like this before," he told Mei Soong.

Mei Soong sat across the white table cloth from him, at last silent. She had denied everything of course. She had not received any messages from Liu's captors. She didn't know where the little red book in her room had come from. She denied being told to lure Remo to the karate school.

She denied this while walking to the restaurant. She denied it while on her way to the ladies room in the restaurant, where she received her instructions from an old Chinese woman. She denied all this even as she placed her order for beef in oyster sauce, and she denied it as she suddenly lost her appetite and let Remo eat the entire dish.

Remo kept eating, just waiting for whatever would come out of the walls. They had gone through four major assaults and now, whoever held General Liu captive, must strike openly. The poor old bastard. Probably in a dungeon someplace, and now betrayed by his wife. Perhaps it was his age that had turned the girl against him. Or perhaps, it as Chiun had said:

"Treachery is the basic nature of a woman."

Remo's answer had been typically thoughtful. "You're

full of crap. What about mothers? Many women aren't treacherous."

"And there are cobras that will not bite. I will tell you why women are treacherous. They are of the same species as men. Heh, heh."

He had chuckled the way he had just chuckled when leaving the table for the kitchen to make sure his food did not contain cats, dogs, Chinese and other vermin.

"The beef in oyster sauce is especially nice, isn't it?" Mei Soong said, as Remo finished up the last morsel.

A sense of warmth overcame him, then a deep feeling of well being and an extreme relaxation of his muscles. The air bloomed with cool smells and Mei Soong's delicate beauty entranced his entire body. The imitation leather seats became pillows of air, and the dark green walls with white pictures became dancing lights, and all was well with the world because Remo had been poisoned.

Before it became too dark, Remo reached out to say goodbye to Mei Soong, a little gesture like putting his left forefinger into her eyesocket to take her with him. He was not sure that he reached her however, because suddenly he was going into a very deep and dark place which spun people around and never let them go. And the oyster sauce was rising back up through his throat into his mouth. That delicious oyster sauce. He would have to get the recipe some day.

* * *

The cook, of course, was giving Chiun lip. Answering back heatedly about the quality of his food until he was made reasonable and responsible and polite, by a pan of hot grease which had, by some mysterious force, sent hot steaming droplets at the cook's arrogant face.

But no one responded to investigate the cook's frenzied yelling. Chiun decided to investigate this. Where was everyone?

He moved from the kitchen, testing the hinges on the swinging doors by seeing how fast the doors could give way to a tray-laden waiter going through them. They gave way very fast, and Chiun pretended to be even more aged than he was when he stepped over the pile of broken dishes out into the main dining hall of the Imperial Gardens. Remo and Mei Soong were gone.

Would Remo leave him like this?

Of course, he would. The child liked to do things like this and often did inexplicable things. Then again, he might have recieved a message which he knew would be Chiun's signal to terminate him. What fools the white men. To have Chiun terminate what was undoubtedly the finest Caucasian on the earth. Would they ask him to terminate Adrian Kantrowitz or Cardinal Cook or Billy Graham or Leontyne Price? People of no value at all?

No. They would ask him to terminate Remo. The fools. But that was the nature of white men. Why, in just thirty or forty years, Remo probably could come close to Chiun, and if he discovered some locked-up hidden power, might even surpass him.

But would the white man wait thirty years? Oh, no. Thirty years was forever to a white man.

A waiter walked up and stood between Chiun and Remo's table. Chiun removed the waiter from his vision, by putting him in a seat. With a broken shoulder. Then Chiun saw the brownish spit on the side of the tablecloth where Remo had been sitting. He asked the waiter where Remo had gone. The waiter said he did not know.

In the mirrors over the front entrance door, Chiun saw a group of men in Chinese waiters' garb spill out of a side door into the main dining area, heading for him.

They did not come to offer assistance. They came to make people uncomfortable. Two of them immediately stopped making Chiun uncomfortable, because they had to attend to their lungs. Their lungs needed attention because they had been punctured by their ribs.

Patrons screamed and huddled against the formica walls

of dining booths, as one man came racing at Chiun waving a cleaver over his head. He kept going. So did the cleaver. So did his head. His head rolled. His body gushed blood all the way to the crowd that suddenly was not a crowd. The cleaver landed onto a table next to a tureen of won ton soup. The head rolled to a stop at the feet of the vice president of the Mamaroneck Hadassah.

And into the din, beyond all voices, spoke Chiun:

"I am the Master of Sinanju, fools. How dare you?"

"No," screamed the waiter and huddled fearfully into a corner of the booth.

"Where is my child that you have taken from me?"

"What child, oh, Master of Sinanju?" said the cowering waiter.

"The white man."

"He is dead of fatal essences."

"Fool. Do you think his body would entertain them? Where is he?"

With his good arm, the waiter pointed to a wall with a large relief of the city of Canton.

"Wait here and speak to no one," Chiun ordered. "You are my slave."

"Yes, Master of Sinanju."

To the bas relief went Chiun, and through its interlocking mechanism went the terrible swift hand, ignited in all the fury of its art. But there was no one left in the restaurant to see him. Only the terrified slave who sobbed in a corner. And he, of course would wait for his master. The Master of Sinanju.

* * *

General Liu saw his loved one coming down the passageway in the dank hallway with the rest of the group, the old Chinese man and two waiters bearing the impossible one.

He had been waiting, hearing the minute by minute reports of the message given, the poison served, the poison

168

eaten, and then an eternity before the impossible one passed out.

Now it was all worth it. He was captured and would soon be dead. And she was here. The delicate, fragrant blossom. The one sweet joy of his hard and bitter life.

"Mei Soong," he said, and brushed past the scurrying water waiters and past the old man. "It's been so long, darling."

Her lips were moist with American lip paste, her dress was of frail material which clung more luxuriously to her young vibrant body. General Liu clutched her to his chest and whispered, "Come with me. It has been so long."

The old Chinese man, seeing the general trundle off with his wife, called out: "What shall we do with this one, comrade general?" and rubbed his hands nervously. The air was very hot in the passageway. He could scarcely breathe.

"He's half dead already. Finish him off." And the general disappeared into his little room, tugging Mei Soong along behind him.

Then the old Chinese man was in the hall way with the white man held up by the two waiters. He nodded to an adjacent door, and drew from his pocket a ring of many keys. Finding one special key, he inserted it in the lock of the wooden door.

It opened easily, revealing a small chamber and an altar lit by flickering candles. A pale porcelain Buddha sat content at the apex of the altar. The room smelled of incense, burned in the memory of years of incense and daily devotions.

"On the floor," said the old man. Put him on the floor. And say nothing of this room to anyone. Do you understand? Say nothing."

When the waiters had left, shutting the door tightly behind them, the old man went to the altar and bowed once.

There were always new philosophies in China but always there was China, and if the new regime looked scornfully upon devotions to gods other than material dialectics, still it would accept the other gods one day, just as all the new regimes eventually accepted all the old gods of China.

Mao was China today. But so was Buddha. And so were the ancestors of the old man.

From his suit pocket, he removed a small dagger and returned to where the white man lay. Perhaps the night tigers of Sinanju were of gods no more, and the master gone with them, and Shiva, the white Destroyer, come and gone where all had gone before.

It was a fine knife, of steel from the black forests of Germany, sold by a German major for many times its worth in jade when the Germans and the Americans and the Russians and the British and the Japanese buried their differences to press the face of China further into the mud.

The major had given the knife. Now, the old man would return it to the white race blade first. The black wooden handle was wet in his palm as the old man pressed the point to the white throat. He would plunge it straight in, then rip to one side, then rip to the other, and then step away to watch the blood flow.

The face seemed strangely strong in its sleep, the eyes deep behind their closed lids, the lips thin and well-defined. Was this the face of Shiva?

Of course not. He was about to die.

"Father and grandfather, and for your fathers and their fathers before them," the old man intoned. "For the indignities upon indignities suffered from these barbarians."

The old man knelt so that he would bring the full force of his shoulder behind the blade. The floor was hard and cold. But the face of the white man was growing pink, then red, as though filled with blood before blood was spilled. A brownish line formed between the thin lips. The old man looked closer. Was it his imagination? He seemed to feel the heat of the body about to die. The line became a dark brown dot on the lower lip, then an elongated puddle that flowed to the sides, then a stream, and then a gush as the face turned red and the body heaved, and out, coming out on the floor, out of the body's system was the oyster sauce and the beef and with it, the poison essences, mixed with the body's fluid and smelling like oysters and vinegar. The man should have been dead. He should have been dead. But his body was rejecting the poison.

"Aiee," screamed the old man," it is Shiva the destroyer."

With a last desperate effort, he raised the knife for the most forceful plunge he could effect. A last chance was better than none at all. But at the knife's apex, a voice filled the basement in thunder.

"I am the Master of Sinanju, fools. How dare you? Where is my child whom I have made with my heart and with my mind and with my will? I have come for my child. How will you die? Now you shall fear death because it is the death brought by the Master of Sinanju."

Outside the door to the little room, servants were screaming directions. "There, there. He is in there."

The old man did not wait.

The dagger came down swiftly and hard, with all his strength. But it did not plunge straight down. Instead, it created an arc to his own heart. It was pain and hot and shocking to his essence. But it was true to its mark and of all his pain, all the pain would not be so bad as punishment from the Master of Sinanju. He tried to twist the knife further into his own heart as his body trembled. But he could not. And it was not necessary. He saw the cold stone floor coming toward him and he prepared to greet his ancestors.

* * *

Remo came to with a bony knee in his back. He was facing the floor. Someone had vomited on the floor. Someone had also bled on the floor. A hand was slapping his neck sharply. He attempted to spin, cracking the slapper in the groin to render him harmless. When he was unable to do this, he knew it was Chiun slapping him.

"Eat, eat. Gobble like a pig. You should have died, it would have taught you a most lasting lesson."

"Where am I?" said Remo.

Slap. Slap. "Why should one who eats like a white man care?"

Slap. Slap.

"I am a white man."

Slap. Slap. "Do not remind me, fool. I have already been made painfully aware of that. Do not eat slowly. Do not taste your food. Gobble. Gobble like a buzzard. Stick your long beak into the food and inhale." Slap. Slap.

"I'm okay now."

Slap. Slap. "I give you the best years of my life and what do you do?"

Remo had raised himself to his knees. Momentarily, during the pounding on his neck, he thought he could perhaps get a sidehand crack at Chiun's jaw, but abandoned the notion. So he let Chiun slap away until Chiun was satisfied that Remo was breathing properly again.

"And what do you do? After all my careful teaching? Hah. You eat like a white man."

"It was really great beef in oyster sauce."

"Pig. Pig. Pig." The word came with the slaps. "Eat like a pig. Die like a dog."

Remo saw the old man lying face down in a layer of blood, that was already darkening about the edges.

"You do the old man?" he asked.

"No. He was smart."

"He looks it," Remo said.

"He understood what would happen. And chose the wise course."

"Nobody as smart as you Orientals."

With a last ringing slap, Chiun finished his work. "Stand up," he ordered. Remo rose, feeling like the pavement during the Indianapolis 500. He blinked his eyes, breathed deeply a few times. And felt quite fine.

"Ecch," he said, noticing the stains of vomit on his shirt. "They must have had knockout drops in the food."

"It is lucky for you," lied Chiun, "that it was not a deadly poison. For if you thought you could survive poison, you would never end your foolish eating ways."

"It was deadly poison, then," Remo said smiling.

"It was not," Chiun insisted.

Remo smiled broadly, straightened his tie, and glanced around the room. "This the basement of the restaurant?"

"Why? Are you hungry?"

"We've got to find Mei Soong. If she's with the general, she might be trying to kill him right now. She's one of them, remember. And the general's in danger."

Chiun gave an abrupt snort, opened the door, and stepped over the two bodies lying outside in a hallway that smelled of musk. Remo noticed that the wooden door had been splintered away from its lock.

Chiun moved like silence in the dark, and Remo followed as he had been taught, in sideways steps along the corridor, in perfect rhythm with the old man before him.

Remo stopped when Chiun stopped. In electric fast movement, Chiun's hand snapped against a door which flung open, momentarily blinding Remo with the light from within. On a plain cot, the hard, yellow, muscled back of a man was on the rise. Two young legs wrapped around his waist. His black hair was crossed with white. Remo saw the soles of Mei Soong's feet.

"Quick, Chiun," he said. "Think of something philosophical."

The man's head spun around in shock. It was General Liu.

"Uh, hello," Remo said.

Chiun spoke, "Have you no shame? Get dressed."

General Liu unplugged with speed and lunged for a .45 caliber automatic on the plain wooden chair. Remo was at the chair in a flash, catching General Liu's arm at the wrist and righting him so he would not fall.

"We're friends," Remo said. "That woman has be-

173

trayed you. She is in league with those who captured you and held you prisoner."

Mei Soong rose on her arms, a look of surprise, then of terror on her face. "Untrue," she screamed.

Remo turned to her, and since the movement of the .45 automatic was not to him, he did not respond with automatic movement, but then heard the crack as he saw the top of her head blasted into the stone wall, splattering blood and gray matter, leaving her brain like a coddled egg about to be eaten from the shell of her skull.

He snatched the gun from General Liu.

"She betrayed me," said General Liu, trembling. Then he fell down and sobbed.

It would not be until he strolled a Peking street that Remo would realize that the general's tears were from relieved tension, and that indeed, Remo had been a very poor detective. He watched Liu fall to his knees and bring his hands to his face, heaving, sobbing.

"Poor bastard. All this and then his wife betraying him too," Remo whispered to Chiun.

Chiun responded with a phrase carrying a very special meaning. "Gonsa shmuck," he said.

"What?" said Remo, not really hearing.

"In English, that means very much a shmuck."

"Poor bastard," said Remo.

"Shmuck," said Chiun.

CHAPTER TWENTY-FOUR

The President's heart was lighter as he watched the newscast. His closest advisor watched also, twisting an index finger through his kinky blond hair.

They sat in the office in deep leather chairs. The President's shoes were off and he twiddled his toes on the hassock. To the right of his left big toe was the advisor's face on the television screen, saying that he would make a trip to Peking and accompany the Premier back to the United States.

"The trip is carefully planned and thorough. Everything will be routine," the voice intoned on TV.

"A routine bit of incredible luck," the President interjected.

A reporter asked the TV face a question. "Will events in China now influence the trip?" he said.

"The Premier's journey is proceeding according to schedule and plans. What is happening in China now influences it in no way."

The President framed his advisor's face between his two big toes. "Now that General Liu is returning with you."

The advisor smiled and turned to the President: "Sir, just how did we find General Liu? The FBI, the CIA, Treasury, everyone says they had nothing to do with it. The CIA wants to guard him now."

"No," the President said. "They will all be busy trying to track down those two men who kidnapped the general. The General will go back to Peking with you. He will be with two men. They will take the rear of your plane."

"I take it you have some special agents I know nothing about."

175

"Professor. Once I could have answered that question. Today, I'm not even sure. And that's all I can say." The President glanced at his watch. "It's almost eight o'clock. Please go now."

"Yes, Mr. President," said the aide, arising with his briefcase. They shook hands and smiled. Perhaps peace, a realistic peace, might yet be achieved by man. Wishing or running rampant in parks with peace symbols would not bring it, however. It would come if one worked and schemed and plotted for peace, just as one did for victory in war.

"It looks good, Mr. President," the aide said.

"It looks good. Good night."

"Good night sir," said the aide and left. The white door shut behind him. And the President listened as various people spoke of Phase Two of his economic Policy. There were five people with five different opinions. It sounded like a meeting of his economic advisors. Well, it was a great country and no President could do it much harm.

The second hand on his watch circled the six and headed up past the seven and nine and eleven, then met the twelve, and there was no ring. God Bless you, Smith, wherever you are, thought the President.

Then the special line rang, like a symphony of bells, and the President hopped from his chair and soft-footed it to his desk. He picked up the receiver on the special phone.

"Yes," he said.

"In answer to your question of two days ago, sir," came the lemony voice, "we will continue but under different circumstances. Something didn't work. I will not tell you what, but it did not work. So in the future, do not even bother to ask for the use of that person."

"Is there some way we can let him know of his nation's gratitude."

"No. As a matter of fact, he is incredibly lucky to be alive."

"I have seen pictures of him from agents tailing Mei

176

Soong. One of them was killed in a karate school. Your man was seen."

"It will not matter. He will not look like that any longer after he returns."

"I do wish there was some recognition, some reward we could give him."

"He's alive, Mr. President. Is there anything else you wish to discuss?"

"No, no. Just tell him thank you from me. And thank you for letting him deliver the general safely to his destination."

"Goodbye, Mr. President."

The President hung up the phone. And he chose to believe, because he wanted to believe, that America still had men like Smith and the man who worked for Smith. The Nation produced men like that. And it would survive.

CHAPTER TWENTY-FIVE

Remo was uncomfortable.

Peking was making him edgy. Everywhere he and Chiun went with their escorts, people noticed them, and stared. Now it was not the noticing that made him uncomfortable, not that. Their eyes were telling him something, even in the crowded shopping areas, the broad pin-neat streets. But he didn't know what.

And something else was bothering him. They had delivered Genaral Liu and received thanks. Two Chinese generals of Liu's Army had looked at Remo very closely and mumbled with Liu. And one of them had said, in obviously mistaken English, "Destroyer . . . Shiva," which was probably a Navy captain or something.

And that afternoon, they would formally be shown the Working People's Palace of Culture, in the Forbidden City, as a special honor.

Chiun was unimpressed with the honor. He had been noticeably cool ever since Remo had expressed heartfelt hurt that Chiun would kill him. Chiun was emotionally distressed that Remo would take it that way.

It had come to a head after Remo had telephoned Smith to tell him the mission was successful. Smith had been silent for a long moment, and then had ordered Remo to tell Chiun his blue butterflies had arrived.

"Can't you think of a better signal than that?" Remo had asked.

"It's for your own good. Inform Chiun of that."

So that afternoon in their hotel room, Remo thought he would bite the bullet once and for all, and see what happened. He was not totally unprepared to take on

Chiun, given, of course, that nothing he had been taught would be new to Chiun and that Chiun's attack would be based on that. But Remo had a secret weapon, one the old man might not expect. A right cross to the jaw, as taught in the CYO boxing team of Newark, New Jersey. Not a perfect weapon, but it might have a chance.

He readied himself in the middle of the room to make Chiun come to him. Then he said softly, "Chiun, Smith says your blue butterflies have arrived."

Chiun was sitting in the lotus position watching the television set, absorbed in whether a young doctor should tell the mother of a leukemia victim that her daughter had leukemia, an especially difficult task because the doctor had once had an affair with the woman and was not sure if it was his daughter or the daughter of Bruce Barlow who owned the town in which they all lived, and who had just contracted a venereal disease, possibly from Constance Lance whom the doctor's stepfather was engaged to, and who had a weak heart which any shock might destroy. Besides, Barlow, as Remo had gathered from two days of that pap, was considering a gift to the hospital to buy a kidney machine which Dolores Baines Caldwell needed desperately if she were to live to finish her study of cancer before her laboratory was repossessed by an as-yet-to-be-introduced Davis Marshall whom the leukemia victim had met on a holiday in Duluth, Minnesota.

"Chiun," Remo repeated, ready to see the last of the world in a sterile hotel with air like ice and bed spreads of drab white ruffles, "Smith says your blue butterflies have arrived."

"Yes, good," Chiun said without looking up from the set. Remo waited for the show to end but Chiun still did not move. Did he want to catch Remo in his sleep?

"Chiun," Remo said as Vance Masterson pondered with James Gregory, district attorney, the fate of Lucille Grey and her father, Peter Fenwick Grey, "your butterflies are in."

"Yes, yes," Chiun said. "You've said that three times. Quiet."

"Isn't that the signal for you to kill me?"

"No, it's the signal for me not to kill you. Quiet."

"So you would have killed me."

"I will kill you now with pleasure if you do not silence your mouth."

Remo walked over to the television set and with the edge of his hand cracked the back of the tube and Chiun sat horrified as the picture sucked itself into a dot of light, then disappeared. Remo dashed out of the room and down the long hallway. On a straightaway, he could beat Chiun. He scrambled down a flight of stairs, along a hallway, and stopped near an open window and laughed until he cried. He sneaked back to the room that evening, and Chiun was sitting in the same position.

"You are a man without heart or soul," Chiun said. "Or intelligence. Angered by the truth of what you know should be true, you foolishly take vengeance on someone who would do something that would be more painful to him than his own death. And neglectful, because I am left to guard the general in the next room and you should be doing that."

"You mean you would rather die than kill me?" Remo asked.

"And that makes you feel better? I do not understand you," Chiun had said. And he had been cold and distant all the way to Peking.

Now, on a Peking street, Remo realized what was bothering him about the peoples' stares. "Chiun," he said. "Stay here and watch me. Tell the guards to stay with you."

Remo did not wait. He hitched his casual blue woolen sweater down over his light tan slacks and walked casually into the main thoroughfare with its occasional cars, its shop windows, under giant posters with Chinese characters, past the rows of Mao pictures, then walked directly back to Chiun and the two guides. One of the guides was on the pavement, his hands to his groin. The other was smiling politely and desperately.

"He said you couldn't be allowed to go alone," Chiun said, nodding at the man in pain on the ground.

"Were you watching?" Remo asked.

"I saw you."

"Did you watch the people?"

"If you mean, did I realize that your theory of General Liu's disappearance in the Bronx was ridiculous, correct. No two men took him anyplace. They would have been seen. He disappeared alone. And like you, just now, aroused no interest at all."

"Then if he disappeared alone. . . .?"

"Of course," Chiun said. "Didn't you know that? I knew it immediately."

"Why didn't you tell me?"

"Interfere with Chief Ironsides, Perry Mason, Martin Luther King, William Rogers and Freud?"

So, thought Remo, Liu had not been kidnaped. He had ordered the drivers off at Jerome Avenue. Then shot them. Then walked away from the car, caught the train and met his cohorts in Chinatown. He had sent people after Remo because Remo had represented the one threat to his plan to sabotage the President's trip. And he had killed Mei Soong, who had known about it, before she could spill what she knew. And now he was back in Peking, a bigger hero and a bigger threat than ever.

"The question is, Chiun, what do we do?"

"If you wish my advice, it is this: mind your own business and let the world of fools hack themselves to death."

"I expected that from you," Remo said. Maybe he could tell someone with the American mission. But no one on the mission knew him. All they knew was that he had return tickets for two to Kennedy Airport and was not to be bothered.

Perhaps call Smith? How? He had enough trouble trying to call him from New York City.

Leave it for the Chinese to settle. But it galled him, right to the gut, it galled him. The son of a bitch shot his wife, and didn't care that millions might die in another war. He wanted this. That was bad. But worse was that he dared to do it. That he thought he had a right to do it, and that bothered Remo deep into his soul.

He looked around the wide clean street with drably-dressed people scurrying to their trivia of the moment. He looked at the clear China sky, unshrouded by air pollution because the people had not yet advanced enough to pollute the air, and thought that if Liu had his way, they never would be granted the gift of dirty air.

Chiun was right of course. But because he was right did not make it right. It was wrong.

"You're right," Remo said.

"But you do not feel that way in your soul, do you?"

Remo didn't answer. He looked at his watch. It was almost time to return for their grand tour of the Working People's Palace of Culture.

General Liu's aide, a colonel, had stressed what an honor it was. The Premier himself would be there to meet the rescuers of the people's general, the colonel had said.

Chiun's advice on that subject was "watch your wallet."

The Forbidden City was truly a spendor. Remo and Chiun and their two guards walked past the stone lion guarding the Gate of Heavenly Peace, for 500 years the main entrance to the city which had once housed emperors and their courts.

They walked across the vast cobbelstone plaza toward the yellow pagoda roofed building which now housed the main museum but which had been a throne room. In a section of the plaza off to their left, Remo saw young and old men exercising in the highly disciplined moves of T'ai Chi Ch'uan, the Chinese version of karate.

The building was beautiful. Even Chiun, for once, had nothing slanderous to say. But its contents reminded Remo of one of those New York auction houses that seem to be devoted exclusively to large and ugly porcelain figures. He did not listen to the rambling explanations of dynasties or thrones or vases or clumsy looking objects, all of which showed that China had discovered this or that or something else way back when Remo was still painting himself blue.

By the time they reached the central vault where General Liu and the Premier waited for them, Remo had been verbally painted blue with enough coats to lather a Celtic army.

Standing in the central vault under the fifty foot high ceiling, the Premier looked like a display porcelain. He was more frail than his pictures. He wore a plain gray Mao suit, buttoned to his neck, but while the suit was plain, the tailoring was immaculate.

He smiled and offered a hand to Remo: "I have heard much about you. It is a privilege to meet you."

Remo refused the hand. "To shake hands," he said, "is to show that I have no weapons. To shake hands therefore would be a lie." The hell with him. Let him and Liu play their goddam war games with the President's staff; they got paid to deal with these devious bastards.

"Perhaps someday, no one will have to bear a weapon," said the Premier.

"In that case, it will no longer be necessary to shake hands to show you have no weapon," Remo said.

The Premier laughed. General Liu smiled. He looked younger in his uniform, but then, that was the reason for uniforms. To make the nasty business of killing impersonal and institutional, something separate from men and pain and all the other hassles of day to day life.

"With the Premier's permission," said General Liu, "I would like to show our guests a most interesting exhibit. I hope you two gentlemen do not mind that we have soldiers present but the Premier must be protected at all costs."

Remo noticed on a narrow step a few feet away were eight soldiers, all of them seeming rather old for the privates' uniforms they were wearing. They had their guns trained on Remo and Chiun. Well, sweetheart, Remo thought, that's the biz.

General Liu nodded with stiff politeness and walked to a glass case, containing a stone-encrusted sword. His leather shoes made clacking sounds on the marble floor and his holster slapped against his side as he walked. The room itself was chilly and badly lighted, blocking out the sunlight and its joy.

"Gentlemen," said General Liu. "The sword of Sinanju."

Remo looked at Chiun. His face had no expression, just an eternal calm that hid wells deeper than Remo's reasoning.

It must have been a ceremonial sword of some sort, Remo thought, because not even a Watusi could wield a sword seven feet long, and flaring out to become as wide as a face, before it came abruptly to a point. The handle was encrusted with red and green stones. It appeared as unwieldly as a wet sofa. If a man's hands were tied to that weapon, you could spit him to death, Remo thought.

"Do you gentlemen know the legend of Sinanju?" General Liu asked. Remo could feel the Premier's eyes upon them.

Remo shrugged. "It's a poor village, I know that. Life is hard there. And you people never treated them very fairly." Remo knew Chiun would love that.

"Truth," said Chiun.

"But do you know the legend? Of the Master of Sinanju?"

"I know," said Chiun, "that he was not paid."

"This sword," said General Liu, "is the sword of the Master of Sinanju. There was a time when China, weak under the monarchistic system, hired mercenaries."

"And did not pay them," said Chiun.

"There was one master of Sinanju who left this sword after slaughtering slaves and then a favorite concubine of the Emperor Chu Ti."

184

Out of the side of his mouth, Remo whispered to Chiun: "You didn't tell me about the nookie."

"He was assigned the concubine and was not paid," Chiun said aloud.

General Liu went on. "The emperor, realizing how foreign mercenaries were destructive to the Chinese people, banished the Master of Sinanju."

"Without paying him," said Chiun.

"Since then we have prided ourselves in never asking for the services of the Master of Sinanju or his night tigers. But imperialists will hire any scum. Even create the destroyer for their evil designs."

Remo saw the smile disappear from the Premier's face as he looked at General Liu with questioning.

"In a society where the newspapers function as an arm of the government, word of mouth becomes the believable truth," said General Liu. "Many people believe that the Master of Sinanju is here, brought by the Imperialist Americans. Many believe he has brought Shiva, the Destroyer, with him. Many people believe that the American imperialists do not seek peace but war. That is why they have sent the Master of Sinanju and his creation to kill our beloved Premier."

Remo noticed Chiun look to the Premier. There was a slight shake of Chiun's head. The premier remained cool.

"But we will kill the paper tigers of Sinanju who have killed our Premier," General Liu said, raising a hand. The riflemen on the balconies aimed their weapons. Remo looked for a display case to dive under.

Chiun said, looking at the Premier: "The last Master of Sinanju to stand in this palace of emperors was not paid. I will collect for him. Fifteen dollars American."

The Premier nodded. General Liu, still holding one hand in the air, took his pistol from its holster with the other.

Chiun laughed then, a resounding, shrieking laugh.

"Rice farmers and wall builders, hear you now. The Master of Sinanju will teach you death." The words

185

echoed through the high ceilinged chamber, bouncing hollowly off the walls and corners and coming back, until it seemed as if the voice came from everywhere.

Suddenly, Chiun became a blurred line, his white robes swirling about him as he moved toward the Premier, then left across General Liu's line of fire. And then the glass case was shattered and the sword seemed to fly into the air with Chiun attached.

The sword swished and blurred with Chiun, whose voice rose maniacally in ancient, high-pitched chants. Remo was about to dart up to the step to go after one of the riflemen and work from there, when he noticed the guns were no longer pointing at him or at the Premier or at Chiun.

Two men clung loosely to their weapons, one whose pants showed a dark wide blotch, growing wider. The other just trembled, his face whitening. Another was vomiting. Four had run. Only one still aimed his rifle but the butt was pressed firmly to a shoulder that had no neck, just a round, dark gushing wound where a head had been. Remo spotted the head, one eye still squinting, rolling to the base of a cabinet where it stopped rolling and stopped squinting. And the sword, now dripping blood, spun faster and faster in Chiun's hands.

The Premier's face was impassive as he stood, his hands folded in front of him. General Liu squeezed off two shots which chipped into the marble floor then bounced into walls with dull thumps, sounding through the museum. Then he stopped squeezing shots, because where his trigger finger had been, there was only a red stump.

And then the hand itself and the pistol were gone as the sword continued to whistle through the air with Chiun seeming to dance under it.

And then, with a shriek, Chiun was without the giant sword. He stood motionless, his arms at his sides, and Remo heard the sword whirring above him, toward the ceiling. Remo looked up. The sword seemed hung in history just a breath from the ceiling, and then it descended, the giant blade turning slowly, until in one last grace-ful turn, it come down into Liu's looking up face.

With a whunk, it split the face and drove straight down through the body, stopping only a foot from the hilt. The clean tip of the blade nicked marble, and then began to gather blood from above. It looked as if General Liu had swallowed too completely the seven foot sword of Sin-anju.

In awesome silence, he tottered, then backward fell, skewered on a sword, creating small flowing lakes of blood around him on the gray marble floors. The hilt seemed to grow from his face.

"Fifteen dollars American," said the Master of Sinanju to the Premier of the latest China. "And no checks."

The Premier nodded. So he was not part of the plot. He was one of the peacemakers. In blood was peace some-times baptized.

"Sometimes, according to Mao," said the Premier, "it is necessary to pick up the gun to put down the gun."

"I'll believe it when I see it," said Remo.

"About us?" asked the Premier.

"About anyone," Remo said.

They escorted the Premier to a car outside and Chiun anxiously whispered to Remo:

"Was my wrist straight?"

Remo, who had barely seen Chiun, let alone his wrist, answered, "Sloppy as hell, little father. You embarrassed me no end, especially in front of the Premier of China."

And Remo felt good.

Watch for

TERROR SQUAD

the next AUTHORS' CHOICE BEST OF THE DESTROYER
from Pinnacle Books

coming in March!

CELEBRATING 10 YEARS IN PRINT
AND OVER 22 MILLION COPIES SOLD!

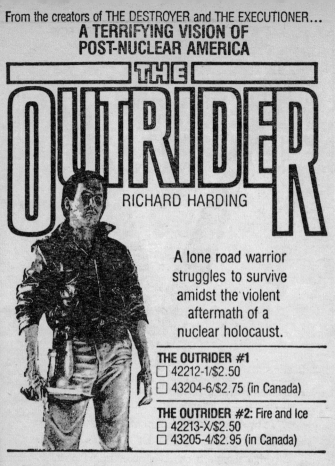